"We can have lunch at the cafe in Hope."

"You don't have to do that."

Cameron glanced Laurel's way before pulling from his parking space. "I don't mind."

"I think you do."

He sighed. "I think you like to argue."

At that she laughed. "I guess maybe I do."

"When I moved into the cottage at Gladys's, I knew she'd push me from my comfort zone."

"Yes, she is a force to be reckoned with."

"But so are you."

Surprise flickered through her hazel eyes. "Me? I'm not a force. I'm the least forciest of people."

He laughed at that. "Oh, you're a force alright. Kittens, Christmas trees, trips to the nursing home."

"I'm not making you do those things," she reminded him.

How well he knew that. The problem was that she didn't have to force him out of his den—he came willingly for her. He used his music to soothe his horses or to gentle an unexpectedly shy or difficult animal. She was the music.

And that was probably the most dangerous thought he'd had in a long time.

Brenda Minton lives in the Ozarks with her husband, children, cats, dogs and strays. She is a pastor's wife, Sunday-school teacher, coffee addict and is sleep deprived. Not in that order. Her dream to be an author for Harlequin started somewhere in the pages of a romance novel about a young American woman stranded in a Spanish castle. Her dreams came true, and twenty-plus books later, she is an author hoping to inspire young girls to dream.

Jill Kemerer writes novels with love, humor and faith. Besides spoiling her mini dachshund and keeping up with her busy kids, Jill reads stacks of books, lives for her morning coffee and gushes over fluffy animals. She resides in Ohio with her husband and two children. Jill loves connecting with readers, so please visit her website, jillkemerer.com, or contact her at PO Box 2802, Whitehouse, OH 43571.

Western Christmas Wishes

Brenda Minton
and
Jill Kemerer

H HARLEQUIN® LOVE INSPIRED®

Recycling programs for this product may not exist in your area.

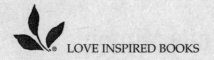

LOVE INSPIRED BOOKS

ISBN-13: 978-1-335-47951-8

Western Christmas Wishes

Copyright © 2019 by Harlequin Books S.A.

The publisher acknowledges the copyright holders of the individual works as follows:

His Christmas Family
Copyright © 2019 by Brenda Minton

A Merry Wyoming Christmas
Copyright © 2019 by Ripple Effect Press, LLC

www.Harlequin.com

Printed in U.S.A.

CONTENTS

HIS CHRISTMAS FAMILY

Brenda Minton

This book is dedicated to my children.

I pray you always follow your dreams,
are always willing to accept a challenge,
try a new path and trust that God has a plan.

Behold, I will do a new thing; now it shall spring forth; shall ye not know it? I will even make a way in the wilderness, and rivers in the desert.
—*Isaiah* 43:19

Chapter One

The small town of Hope, Oklahoma, happened to be everything Laurel Adams didn't want for Christmas. She didn't want twinkling lights, country cafés decorated with green and-silver garland or people who stood on the street corner and offered a cheery greeting as she drove past. She wanted big-city anonymity and her Chicago apartment, with its view of Lake Michigan. Instead she found herself in a town she had visited only twice in over twenty years.

When she was nine years old, she and her mother had moved from Hope to Chicago. It had been their fresh start, her mom had said. It was their adventure. Really, it had been their escape.

Back then, the town of Hope hadn't been a friendly haven to a single mother who worked as a waitress and did her best to survive. Laurel's grandmother assured her it had changed. As Laurel drove into town, it was easy to see the cosmetic differences. But the surface wasn't what mattered to a girl who had been hurt by names and dirty looks.

You could hang twinkling lights on it, put on a fresh coat of paint and plant flowers. Those things didn't change the heart of a town. You could put a fancy facade on the front of a building, but if the foundation was crumbling, it didn't matter a bit.

She turned on a side road that led along the lake and up into the hills on the northern edge of town. Her grandmother's old Victorian sat on the hillside overlooking the lake. It was a picturesque home, with pale peach siding, sage-green trim and a wraparound porch with white rocking chairs for summer evenings. It hadn't changed since Laurel's not-so-picturesque childhood.

And yet, somehow, it still felt like coming home. She shook off the thought. This wasn't a homecoming; it was a necessary visit. She was here to check on her grandmother.

She parked in the driveway and stepped out. A cold December breeze greeted her and she pulled her jacket closed as she looked around, taking in all that was familiar, as well as what had changed.

There was a caretaker. Laurel wondered where she would find him. She grabbed her purse out of the car, then headed up the stone walkway to the front porch. A shadow shifted and changed, becoming a shaggy brown dog as it exited the woods. The animal barked as he approached.

"Easy, boy. I belong here." Sort of.

The dog continued to bark, his tail wagging but not in quite as friendly a manner as she would have liked. He growled at her, and she froze.

"Zorro, down." A strong, deep and in-command voice called out. The owner of it emerged from the woods—he was tall with a black cowboy hat pulled low on his head.

She remained rooted to the spot, afraid of both the dog and the man walking next to the gigantic animal. As they drew closer she gasped and took a step back.

At her reaction he snapped his fingers and spun to walk away, the dog moving quickly to his side with just a backward glance and one last warning growl.

"Wait," she called to his retreating back. "I'm sorry. I just…"

She was unforgivably rude. She knew how it felt to be judged. As a child she'd suffered the dirty looks, the whispers, the judgment for what her parents had done. She knew how painful it was.

"I was rude and I'm sorry," she called out after him.

He stopped, paused for mere seconds and then turned back, giving her the full effect of his scarred face. The right side was rather beautiful, with lean bone structure, a mouth that formed a straight and unforgiving line, and blue eyes.

Correction. One blue eye. One eye patch.

"Are you finished?" he asked. He meant, was she finished staring.

She took a step closer. "I'm sorry. Truly. I didn't expect anyone to be here. And the dog frightened me."

"And my face, let's not forget my face."

She contemplated her next words carefully. An objection would be a lie, and condescending to boot. He knew the truth so she should speak the truth.

"Okay, yes, you shocked me. But what frightened me was the dog." On a second look, she realized the scars weren't so shocking. The skin on the left side of his face was rough and a defined scar ran along his cheek and down his neck.

"Bravo for honesty." He clapped a slow and steady beat. "Now, if you'll excuse me, I have work to do."

"Wait!" she called out as he started to walk away again.

He stopped.

"Are you the caretaker?"

He laughed, his one blue eye sparkling with genuine humor. "No, I'm not. Is that what Gladys told you?"

"She said I would have to get the key from her caretaker."

"I'm not the caretaker. I rent her guesthouse while my home is being built. But I do have a key to the main house." He gave her a long look with an eye so blue it mesmerized, and thick lashes that only made it more compelling. That piercing gaze somehow made her feel as if the solid ground beneath her would soon give way.

"Also, I'm not a babysitter so please come get Capital T," he said as he started to walk away from her.

"Capital T? Babysitter?" Laurel blinked, trying to decipher what he was saying.

"Rose. She's *Trouble* with a capital *T*. Not my trouble—yours. She's been here all afternoon and I haven't been able to get a hold of Kylie West. So Capital T is here, getting in the way, messing with my horses, annoying my dog. If you'll follow me, you can have the key and the child."

"Child?"

He pinned her with that steady gaze of his.

"Gladys didn't tell you anything, did she?" His hand went to the monstrous dog at his side. Her gaze followed the gesture, the calming hand, the wiry haired black dog that looked as if he could eat a small ham in one bite. Or her leg.

He cleared his throat and she returned her full attention to the owner of the dog.

"I'm afraid I'm in the dark," she told him. "My grandmother just said that she could use some help around here until she gets out of the facility where she's doing her physical therapy and recovery."

"Gladys is one of a kind." There was a hint of admiration in his words, mixed in with a good dose of exasperation. Then he headed for the barn.

"What's your name?" she asked.

"Cameron Hunt."

He didn't ask for her name. She guessed he probably knew. She was Laurel, the granddaughter who should have been here sooner, should have visited more often. She didn't need to be told—she already knew.

She followed him toward the stables. Years ago it had been her grandmother's pride and joy, a metal building with a large corral attached. Beyond were fields that in the spring would be brilliant green, but browned in December. She inhaled the country air, perfumed with the drying grass and damp earth.

As much as she didn't want to feel a connection to this place and her past, she did.

"So, Cameron Hunt, who exactly is Capital T? Other than a child."

He slowed his steps, allowing her to catch up. He was tall and his stride was double hers.

"She's your grandmother's great-niece. Or perhaps great-great-niece. I only know that Gladys has custody and that *Trouble* is her middle name. She's thirteen and in everyone else's business. A lot like your grandmother."

"So you like them?" she asked, trying to hide her humor. She hadn't wanted to be amused, not by him or by the situation.

"I like my privacy," he said in a stilted tone that seemed to be trying a little too hard for gruffness.

She switched topics.

"How did Gladys hurt her shoulder? She wasn't forthcoming with details."

"She didn't tell you?" He shot her a quick look but kept walking. "No. Of course she didn't. She must not want you to know."

"All she said was the how isn't important. What's important is that she's going to get better and get back home as soon as possible."

"She got tossed by that crazy horse of hers. She won't give up and get a decent animal."

"She's eighty! She was riding a horse?"

He stopped walking and stared her down with one piercing blue eye. "You should get to know her."

And then he continued on, leaving her to follow after him, having no defense for her absence from her grandmother's life. She decided to be angry with him. Anger was safer than every other confusing emotion she felt when she looked at him. Guilt. Shame. Attraction. Anger.

Not attraction. Cross that off the list. He annoyed her. That was it. End of story.

Cameron didn't consider himself an impatient person. He thought that thirty-five years on this earth had taught him to be kind, take his time in making judgments and choose his words wisely. For whatever reason, the woman at his side had him forgetting all those things, and scrambling to find his better self.

Maybe Gladys was right. Maybe he'd spent too much time alone. Since his return from Afghanistan, he'd found solace in his lone existence and in his horses. This was his version of healing.

Being alone had worked for him until Gladys had made him her pet project. She had a way of invading a person's life. All of his usual tactics for running people off—growl a little, glare a lot, make himself unavailable for small talk—hadn't worked on Gladys. Or Capital T, as he liked to call Rose.

He spotted the girl inside the stable. His dog spotted her at the same time and loped off to join her.

The city girl tromped along behind him, not quite able to keep up with his longer strides. He smiled, picturing her back there in her high-heeled boots, a knit scarf around her neck and her red hair bouncing around her face. It was cool enough that her hazel eyes would flash and her cheeks would turn a shade of pink that would clash with her complexion.

He stopped when he reached the stable doors and didn't go inside as he'd planned. With an about face, he almost bumped into Gladys's granddaughter as she marched up behind him. He'd been right about how she would look. Her hazel eyes flashed and her cheeks were pink from the cold. He refocused over her shoulder to the view of the lake. From here the view was stunning. In winter the water appeared to be the biblical crystal sea, it was that clear.

"Where is Rose?" the city girl asked, a little out of breath.

"Probably bothering my cat. She had a new litter of kittens and Rose won't leave them alone."

As if on cue, the teen appeared. She had a kitten cuddled against her face but her smile dissolved when she spotted them. Wary dark eyes focused in on their visitor.

"Who is she?" Rose asked, brushing short dark hair back from her face.

"I'm Laurel Adams. Gladys's granddaughter."

"Oh." Rose shot him a look that made him think he'd just gained enemy status. But it hadn't been his idea to call the granddaughter and ask her to come to Oklahoma.

"Gladys sent for me," Laurel informed her.

"I'm not sure why," Rose went on, in Rose-like fashion. Full-throttle, take-no-prisoners, no-holds-barred. That was Rose. "It isn't as if you know her or she knows you. You haven't seen her in ten years."

"Nine," Laurel countered.

"Oh! Nine. That's *so* much better." Rose rolled her eyes heavenward. "I have to take the kitten back to her mother. I've been staying with Kylie West. I'll have to go get my stuff."

"Get your stuff?" Laurel asked, her hands jammed into her pockets.

Rose smirked but then softened the look into a somewhat sympathetic expression. Cameron watched the two of them, wondering when the drama would play out so that he could get back to the horse he'd been working with.

"If you're here, I should probably stay with you. Right?"

Laurel looked a little panicked. "I'm really not sure."

Her gaze shot to him, asking for intervention.

Cameron took a step back. "I raise horses, not teenagers. If I were you, I'd go visit Gladys and find out what she's up to."

"Then that's what we'll do. I'll unload my luggage and then we'll make a trip to town. Oh, I need the key."

"I'll walk you down there. The lock is tricky and there are a few things I should show you." He didn't know why he offered. He could tell her the things she needed to know and the lock wasn't that tricky.

"I'm sure we can manage," she told him.

"Still, I'd rather make sure you're all settled. That'll keep you from knocking on my door at midnight."

Before Laurel could say anything, he started for the path that led back to Gladys's house. Rose caught up with him, walking on his right side because she knew that he preferred to see the person walking next to him. He glanced down, noticing a suspicious movement in her coat pocket, and decided he'd ignore it for now.

But he couldn't ignore the fact that he was getting dragged further and further into Gladys Adams's life. First it had been his elderly neighbor pushing him to attend church. And then Rose had shown up. Now the granddaughter.

The guesthouse, situated down a trail from the main

house, was no longer feeling like the sanctuary it had been when he first moved off Mercy Ranch.

He could have gone anywhere to start his new life but he'd decided to settle in Hope, Oklahoma, the town that had given him a second chance. Jack West and his ranch for wounded warriors had been a huge part of his recovery.

And the place where he'd grown up no longer felt like home. The ranch in Texas had been sold. His siblings had all moved away. He'd needed somewhere to put down roots and rebuild his life.

"Where is the nursing home?" Laurel Adams asked as they neared the house.

"On the highway, heading toward Grove. If you're familiar with the area, it's the road on the right, before the bridge."

Her face scrunched but she didn't say anything, and instead glanced at Rose. If she thought Rose would give her directions, she was wrong. No doubt Rose would lead her on a wild-goose chase.

He pulled the house key out of his pocket and showed Laurel how to turn it while jiggling the door handle. She watched, leaning in close. She smelled good, like herbal shampoo and a light perfume, something not too sweet or heavy. He liked it.

A lot.

He pulled back and handed over the key.

"Is that it?"

"No, you'll need to know where the breaker box is. If you run the dishwasher, microwave and coffeepot at the same time, a breaker will flip. You'll have to reset it."

"I don't plan on it," she said, then nodded and relented. "Okay, go ahead and show me."

Behind them, Rose giggled. He shot her a look and she tried for innocent but then she waggled her eyebrows and glanced at Laurel's back. He shook his head. Rose nodded, and then suddenly remembered the object in her pocket and her hand went back in, protectively covering the kitten she was pretending she didn't have.

He continued guiding Gladys's granddaughter through the house. The tour included information on the tricky breaker box, showing her how to reset the furnace thermostat, then telling her about the stray dog that wasn't Gladys's, but she fed the mongrel, anyway.

Rose occasionally gave him a pointed look and he tried to avoid eye contact with the teenager. When she started jerking her head toward the granddaughter and nodding, he aimed a finger at her to stop her nonsense. He remembered his little sister doing the same thing to him when she thought he ought to like a specific girl.

He was only too glad to bid both of them goodbye and head back to his place. He was on his own again. They were on their own.

Of course it wouldn't be that simple. Christmas was just weeks away and the little town of Hope fairly buzzed with Christmas cheer. Laurel Adams was in his life for at least a week, maybe longer if her meddling grandmother had any say in the matter.

Knowing Gladys the way he did, he knew that Christmas would have its share of surprises.

Chapter Two

"How long are you staying?" the girl in the passenger seat asked without looking at Laurel.

"A week or two."

"Figures."

Laurel kept driving, looking for the turn before the bridge that Cameron Hunt had mentioned. "What does that mean?"

"Aunt Gladys said you wouldn't stay long because the past hurts too much. Or something like that. But I think the past shouldn't be as important as your grandmother. Or maybe you should deal with the past and move on."

Laurel spotted her turn and hit her turn signal. "How old are you?"

"Thirteen." A mew from inside her pocket punctuated the sentence.

"Thirteen and you're a self-designated life coach?"

"Nope, I just know stuff. I've lived a lot of life in thirteen years."

"Yes, well, I'm sure you don't know as much as you think you do. I'm not sure what your problem is, but you can't sit there and diagnose my life." Laurel sighed. She was arguing with a kid.

From the passenger seat, Rose whispered something to the kitten in her pocket.

"What?" Laurel asked, softening her tone.

"You asked what my problem is. A lot of things. I'm difficult, dysfunctional, dyslexic and a lot of other *D* words. Some of them I can't repeat because my mother had a colorful way with words that Aunt Gladys doesn't appreciate." Her tone was dry but there was a brief flicker of pain that Laurel couldn't miss.

"I'm sorry," Laurel said. "Is this the right way?"

It definitely didn't look like the right way and her phone didn't have a signal, so there was no GPS.

"I don't think so."

"Rose, maybe you could give me directions?" she said as she pulled over, just as a red truck drove by. "I'm sure you've visited Gladys and know how to get there. And why do you have a kitten in your pocket?"

Rose grinned and pulled the kitten from her coat. "I've never had a pet."

"You can't just take a kitten. It might need to be with its mother."

"It's six weeks old. They're ready to be weaned. That's what Cameron said last week. If Gladys won't let me keep it, I'll take it back to the mama cat. But I'm going to tell Gladys I got it for her. She won't turn away a gift."

"You think that'll work?"

Rose shrugged. "Worth a shot."

"Good luck with that. Now, how do I get to the nursing home?"

"You're on the right road. It looks like a driveway but it really is a road."

"Thank you."

She put the car in Drive and continued on down the

road. As they rounded a bend, she saw the red truck ahead of them.

"That's Cam's truck," Rose informed her.

"Is it?"

"Yeah, he must have worried that I would get you lost. He acts all grouchy and tough but he's really okay."

"Good to know."

"Pretty cute, too. If you just look at the side without the scars."

"I'm not interested," Laurel informed the teen.

"Right, because you're getting over a bad breakup and you resent men because you never knew your father. I didn't know mine, either, but I don't plan on being single my whole life. I want a husband and kids, a good job, the whole package."

Laurel blinked. "You're a bit of a mess."

"Yeah, well, my mom is your second cousin, Tarin. She's not exactly a role model."

"Where is she these days?" Laurel asked as the brick facility came into view.

"Tarin? Who knows? We were living with a friend of hers in Grove and she took off one night, left me sleeping on their couch. After a few days they called Family Services because I'm not their responsibility. DFS found Gladys and she took me in. My grandmother was Gladys's sister. She passed away years ago."

Laurel had to give it to the girl—she was an optimist. Laurel thought about romance in terms of the father she'd never known because he'd failed to tell her mother he was engaged to someone else. He'd dated her mother on summer break, but his fiancée was the woman he'd met in college.

"You don't know why your mom left?" Laurel asked as she parked.

"Who knows? She's an addict. Aunt Gladys says everyone's an addict these days and who knows what society is coming to. Anyway, Tarin's a rotten mom and a horrible person."

"She's an addict, Rose. She probably didn't plan for that to happen. Sometimes it happens to really good people."

"Yeah, I guess. She told me one time that she was a straight-A student until her junior year, when she fell in with the wrong crowd. One time, one wrong friend, and her whole life changed. I guess I kind of wonder why she doesn't just change it back."

Easier said than done, Laurel thought. But she didn't say it out loud. She'd lost friends to addictions. Knew the devastation it could do to a family. She cleared her throat and moved on, because Rose had a shimmer of moisture in her eyes.

"Hey, there's Cam." Rose opened her door to get out.

Laurel let her go. She knew about deflecting, about changing subjects and trying hard not to let things hurt.

Cameron Hunt waited on the sidewalk in front of the nursing home. Laurel took her time getting out of her car. She wasn't quite ready for this visit. It had been too long since she'd seen her grandmother. Gladys had visited Chicago but her last visit had been for Laurel's college graduation, just over eight years ago. Laurel's mom had visited Hope but Laurel had avoided the town that held too many bad memories.

She'd been a small-town girl whose mom had made a mistake. She knew all about gossip, whispers and dirty looks. Her mom had never told anyone the name of the father of her child. She'd said it didn't matter. But it must have mattered to her, because she'd never married.

"You made it," Cameron said as she got out, joining him on the sidewalk.

Rose was ahead of them, nearly to the front door of the

facility. Laurel let the girl go because she obviously knew her way and hopefully couldn't get into trouble between here and there.

The man walking next to her switched sides, giving her the unscarred side of his face. She started to tell him it wasn't necessary, but she didn't know him well enough to tell him what was or wasn't necessary.

"We made it. I was afraid she would purposely get me lost."

"Your fears were well-grounded," he agreed with a grim look. "I headed this way shortly after you left with Rose, to make sure you found the place. And yet, I beat you here. That must have been you pulled over on the side of the road."

The gesture of kindness surprised her. From the look on his face, it surprised him, as well. He obviously hadn't meant to get involved. After knowing Rose for less than two hours, she could see how the girl would drag someone in, not giving them the opportunity to decide if they wanted to be involved or not.

They were close to the entrance when the door opened and a man exited. Laurel glanced his way, but then she took a longer look as he stopped to talk to Rose. He was tall with dark auburn hair and hazel eyes. Laurel hesitated as the world seemed to spin a little too fast.

"You okay?" Cameron Hunt asked.

She watched as the man, a stranger, turned toward her. He saw her and his smile faltered. He drew in a breath and seemed to hold it.

"I'm good," she lied. "Please go inside with Rose."

She could be wrong, she told herself. He was a stranger with hair a darker shade of red than her own. It meant nothing. The way he looked at her meant nothing.

"I think I should stay here with you." Cameron's hand

was on her arm, steadying her. She thought she didn't need to be steadied but realized that her legs were weak and the world had faded a little. She shook her head to clear the strange fuzziness.

"Laurel?" Cameron's voice seemed to come from far away. And then Rose was next to her, staring at her, looking concerned.

"I'm okay," she assured them.

But she wasn't. The man who had left her mom to be a single mother, the man she'd spent her life resenting, was standing in front of her.

After all of these years of wondering, it had been this simple. The two of them on a sidewalk, instantly recognizing one another. That he was here brought up questions, but those questions weren't for him. They were for her grandmother.

Cameron and Rose disappeared into the building. She stared at the man who had given her red hair and fair skin that burned too easily in the sun. She didn't even know his name.

Her own father and she couldn't call him by name. She didn't know his age, where he lived, what he did for a living. A small voice inside her told her that her mother shared some of the blame for her lack of information regarding her father.

"What are you doing here?" She asked the first question that came to her mind.

He seemed surprised by it.

"I was visiting my mother," he said simply, gently. "I guess I should introduce myself."

"You're about thirty years too late for that." She shifted her gaze away from him, from the sympathy in his expression. A wreath hung on the door of the nursing home, a sign of the coming holidays. Thirty Christmases. Missed.

"Yes, I know." He reached out to her but let his hand drop before touching her. "Your grandmother called me to let me know you'd be in town. She thought that perhaps this would be a good time for us to meet."

"I doubt she meant like this, on the sidewalk, with no one to introduce us."

"No, I'm sure this isn't what she intended." He looked around, as if trying to think of a better plan. It was too late. "We could sit down and talk."

"I don't think so." For years she'd rehearsed what she would say and do if she ever met him. When she'd been younger, she'd dreamed of him walking through the front door and being everything a little girl wanted a daddy to be.

As a teenager those dreams had turned to anger and resentment.

Anger was easier to deal with than disappointment. Anger worked as a shield to keep her heart safe.

He studied her, as if he knew the direction her thoughts had taken.

"Maybe you could think about it and if you change your mind, you can call me. Gladys has my number."

She shook her head. "I have to go inside. My grandmother is expecting me."

He seemed to want to say more, but when she shook her head, he didn't. "I'll leave you for now, but I'll be waiting. I'm praying for you, Laurel."

The words stopped her. Her hand was on the door and she needed to go inside. Rather than saying something she couldn't take back later, she hit the buzzer and waited for the door to unlock. She walked inside, aware that he was still there, watching her walk away.

Ten steps into the building, Cameron Hunt appeared in front of her. She looked up, focusing on the ceiling because she didn't want to cry, not in front of this man, a virtual stranger. She didn't want to cry period.

"You okay?"

She lowered her gaze from the ceiling to the man standing just feet away from her. His expression remained impassive. He didn't want to be involved. And yet here he was.

"I'm good," she assured him, although it didn't feel like the truth. "Did we lose Rose?"

"She's with Gladys." He surprised her by grabbing a box of tissues from a nearby table. "Take a minute. They'll be fine on their own. Hopefully."

She started to object—to the tissues, to taking a moment—but she knew he was right. She took his offering and leaned against the wall as she pulled herself together.

He stood next to her, his back against the paneled wall. His nearness provided an odd sense of comfort, as if he was an ally. It didn't make sense but she wasn't questioning it, not right now when she desperately needed a calming influence.

His presence was the furthest thing from calming. He smelled like mountains and Oklahoma. His boots were dusty and worn. He'd placed himself so that the eye patch and scarred side of his face weren't what she saw when she looked up at him.

The moment was cut short by raised voices and some sort of ruckus.

"Uh-oh," she said as she pushed away from the wall. "That can't be good."

"Doesn't sound that way," he agreed. "Time to intervene. I should have known that the two of them couldn't stay out of trouble."

"It might be someone else."

He turned his head to peer at her with that one startling

blue eye. A flash of humor flickered for an instant. "That is wishful thinking."

"I suppose you're right." She tossed the tissue in a wastebasket. "Thank you."

"For what?"

"For insisting I take a minute to get it together." She hesitated. "Do you know him?"

He pushed back his cowboy hat and gave her a thoughtful look. "You don't know him?"

"I think I know who he is, but I don't know his name."

"Curt Jackson. Local rancher. He just moved back to the area six months ago. His father passed away and his mother couldn't handle the ranch on her own."

Curt Jackson. Thirty years of wondering had come down to this. Suddenly, the ruckus from down the hall grew louder.

"This way." Cameron motioned her forward, his hand just barely skimming her back as he moved her in the right direction.

Seconds later they entered a large room where a variety of people had gathered: staff in scrubs, residents, some standing, some sitting, and a woman at the center who seemed to be in charge of the chaos. She was tall, dressed in a skirt and jacket, her hair pulled back in a tight bun.

The man facing her wore a jogging suit of light gray, the same color as his thinning hair. He was pointing at her with a gnarled finger.

"Are you telling me we can't have a Christmas tree?" he asked.

"I'm sorry, Mr. Clyburn, but the new owner said there will be no Christmas tree in the common area. It isn't my rule, it's the rule of the management."

"Oh, fiddlesticks, Dora, you've been here long enough. You could fight for us."

"I can't fight this. No Christmas tree. Jeremy will take it back to storage." She looked around at the group that had gathered. "I am sorry."

The gentleman in the jogging suit shook his head. "Oh, Dora, what in the world are you thinking? There are folks here who have next to nothing and no family to bring them gifts."

"My hands are tied." She nodded at a man in gray coveralls who had a perplexed look on his face. "Jeremy, please take the tree and decorations back to storage."

The gentleman in the gray jogging suit sat down at a nearby table. "It's a tree. You put lights on it and shiny things."

"Mr. Clyburn, you have to understand, this is not my rule. There will be no religious celebrations anymore, per the new owner."

"There's little enough cheer in this place without you taking it all away." An older woman with curly gray hair and a determined look stepped forward, Rose at her side.

Laurel's grandmother. Gladys Adams hadn't seemed to age. Other than her arm in a sling, she was as spry as ever and obviously as willing to take on the administrator as she was the horse that had thrown her.

"You will still have Christmas dinner." Dora made the announcement, turning right and left so that the dozen people gathered in the room heard her.

"A dinner made of government commodities that they spend almost nothing to purchase," Gladys protested with a grim look of determination.

"Gladys," Dora responded, "it appears you have company."

Laurel smiled and waved at her grandmother.

"That I do," Gladys replied. "And since I'm just here

for physical therapy, I'll be going home soon. The rest of these poor souls have to suffer through your tight budget."

Gladys hurried over to Laurel, hugged her tightly and then allowed herself to be led from the room.

"That didn't sound good, Gran," Laurel observed.

"They're stealing Christmas," Rose chimed in.

"That's a little dramatic, don't you think?" Cameron asked as he came up behind them.

Rose shot him a look. "Of course it is, but I'm all about the *D*'s."

He looked perplexed and Laurel found herself smiling, because she knew about the *D*'s. Her grandmother's hand on her arm made her feel better than she'd felt in weeks. Since her bakery had failed, then she'd learned the man she'd been dating was also dating another woman, *upheaval* seemed to be too calm a word to describe how her life had felt.

For a moment she forgot that a man named Curt Jackson existed and he was more than likely her father. Somehow her quick trip to Hope, a needed visit with her grandmother, had turned more than a little bit complicated.

Cameron Hunt stepped around her, pushing open the door to her grandmother's room. He made quick eye contact with her and she smiled. She would leave in a couple weeks but he would always fill a space in her memories. He'd been the person with her when she met her father for the first time.

Not her mother. Not her grandmother.

This man.

Chapter Three

Cameron stood there awkwardly, watching as Gladys looked her granddaughter over. He should leave. He couldn't even explain why he'd decided to visit today, other than to make sure Laurel and Rose got here safely. Not that they'd needed an escort.

He had things to do. He was building a house. He had horses that needed working while the weather was good. He didn't need to be involved in this reunion. He lived in Hope because the town was peaceful, and he was in need of peace.

"Who is Curt Jackson?" Laurel's question jerked him back to the present. He looked from the younger woman to her grandmother.

Of course, Gladys didn't look shaken. If she could take on a half-broke horse, she could handle a question like that. But then Rose pulled the kitten out from her pocket. Gladys noticed the animal and her eyes widened.

"Is that one of Cam's kittens?" Gladys asked.

Rose immediately put the kitten back in her pocket. "What kitten?"

"I can promise you, young lady, my vision is very good."

Cameron put a hand on Rose's back and gave her a little nudge toward the door. "Let's go find the vending machine."

"Thank you, Cam." Gladys gave him a winning smile.

"Hey, what's up with that?" Rose asked as he guided her down the hallway. "I wanted to visit with Gladys, too."

"I'll buy you a candy bar." He had a suspicion Laurel needed to talk to her grandmother about more than her stay in the nursing home.

"Is that a bribe?"

"It is," he answered.

"It's wrong for them to take away the tree and gifts from these people," Rose told him as they entered the lounge with the vending machines. "I don't think it's about Christmas. I think they're just being cheap."

"I would agree." His guess was that the new owners planned to flip the business and wanted to cut corners and increase profit to make it look like a good investment.

Rose glanced at him after perusing the selection in the vending machine. "We have to do something."

"Not my place," he answered.

"I'll have to come up with my own plan, then." She held her hand out. "Dollar please."

He handed over the money and tried not to worry about Rose coming up with a plan.

"Do you think she's pretty?" she asked.

"Who? Dora?" He pretended ignorance.

"Good try."

"I think she's none of my business," he told the teen. He looked at his watch. "And I have to go."

"Chicken," the girl clucked.

He refrained from rolling his eyes—something a grown man shouldn't even think of doing. "I'm not going to respond to that. I have an appointment with my contractor."

He ignored the look she gave him. He wasn't chicken,

he just needed his space. He needed his horses, a few head of cattle and no awkward looks as people pretended they weren't staring, weren't wondering what had happened to him.

"What about Gladys?" Rose continued, following him down the hall.

"What about her?"

"She has to stay here for twenty days. They'll ruin her Christmas."

"Rose, Gladys isn't going to be here at Christmas. I know Gladys and she'll be done with this place before then."

"She can't just leave, can she? It's like prison. When they put a person in a place like this, they lose their freedom. The doors are locked. Didn't you notice the doors are locked? You're a lawyer, you know how these things work."

"I have a law degree. But I'm not a lawyer."

"Yeah, yeah, your face, and all of that. But you know how it works. Legally they can keep people here."

The girl was truly frightened. He could see it in her eyes. She might try to act like life was all fun and games, but Rose had been through some hard times. Gladys was probably the first properly functioning adult in her young life and she was giving Rose a first taste of a normal and safe home.

"Gladys is here voluntarily. It's a twenty-day program to help her with physical therapy and to regain full use of her arm and shoulder."

"So she can leave? She'll come home?" Rose stood in front of the door, not allowing him to leave. "I won't have to go to a foster home with strangers? Or a group home?"

"Rose, I am not an expert at these kinds of cases, but I think you're safe."

"If they try to take me, will you be my lawyer?"

He pulled his hat low and sighed. "I'm not a lawyer but I'll do what I can to make sure they don't take you from Gladys."

She wrapped her arms around him in a quick hug. "I hope she stays."

"What?" He shook his head at the quick change. "You were just saying you want her out."

"I mean Laurel. I hope she stays. It would be easier for Gladys to keep me if she had help. The caseworker says all the time that Gladys is eighty and probably too old to raise a teenager. If Laurel stays…"

Yeah, yeah, he got it. If Laurel stayed, Rose would be happy. Gladys would be happy. Everyone would be happy. Except Laurel, he suspected.

Cameron needed to get home and focus on his life, instead of getting involved in the lives of these three ladies.

"I should have come down when Mom visited," Laurel inserted. "I'm sorry."

"Life is full of regrets, Laurel. We can't let them eat us up. Instead we make the best of the days we've got. You learn something about that when you take a hair-turning ride on a half-broke horse." She took hold of her granddaughter's arm. "Sit down. I think we have a lot to discuss and Cameron won't be able to contain Rose for very long. The girl has so much energy. Home sweet home. Have a seat."

"It's nice," Laurel offered.

Gladys sat on the straight-back chair near the window. "Oh, it isn't nice. It's necessary. And it's a reason to work hard on my physical therapy and get home."

"I'm sorry," Laurel said as she took a seat on the bed.

"Don't be. I'm glad you're here. If I'd known it took surgery to get you here, I would have tried it sooner."

"Don't."

"I'm kidding." Gladys shifted to pull the blinds closed and block the sun, which had suddenly decided to shine through the window. "How long will you be able to stay?"

"I planned on just over a week."

"I see. Well, I plan on getting out of here as soon as possible. Your mother told me about your bakery."

Of course she had. "Yes, I guess it was the wrong time to start a business."

"It's always iffy when you start up something like that. And I heard about the boyfriend, too."

"It seems you and Mom have talked a lot."

Gladys looked surprised by that. "Well, of course—she's my daughter. We talk several times a week."

She should have known that. Of course her mother and grandmother talked on the phone. Patricia Adams might dislike her hometown but she loved her mother. Her visits to Hope had been more frequent than Laurel's. Since Laurel moved off on her own, her mother had returned each summer to spend a week in Hope.

"So your boyfriend turned out to be a cheater. And your bakery went belly-up. Time to reinvent yourself and start over."

Her mother and grandmother were definitely cut from the same cloth. It was hard to think about starting over when she'd thought the bakery was her new start.

"Has your mother told you that she's thinking about moving here?"

Another bomb dropped without warning. "No, she hasn't. I mean, I think she mentioned it in passing. But she also mentioned Florida. Anywhere warm and away from the city."

"Yes, I know she's considered Florida but lately we've

talked more about her moving here. I should have let her tell you."

"It's okay. I can handle hearing that she might have plans for her future."

"Laurel, I'm just so glad to see you." Gladys reached for her hand. Laurel took the cool, thin fingers in her own and warmed them.

"I'm glad to see you, too, Grandma. Is there anything I can bring you?" She grinned. "Other than a Christmas tree?"

Her grandmother laughed. "You'll get me kicked out of here. But maybe that wouldn't be such a bad thing." She was quiet for a moment, then she sighed. "You could bring me a home-cooked meal."

"I'll bring you lunch tomorrow."

They chatted for several more minutes, then silence. Laurel looked down at her hands, wondering, as she often did, if they were "his" hands, Curt Jackson's. They weren't her mother's. Her mom had long slim fingers. Laurel's fingers weren't long. She had strong hands.

"Is Curt Jackson my father?" she asked without preamble.

"Oh, goodness," Gladys gasped. "Well…"

"He was leaving just as I got here, so I know you probably know he was here."

Gladys nodded. "He was here visiting his mother. She had a stroke not long after his father passed. But the rest, that's something your mother needs to tell you."

"So he *is* my father? Have you always known?"

Gladys shook her head. "No."

Laurel felt like she was falling apart inside. Like everyone she'd counted on had lied to her. They had, she supposed. Probably with good intentions but it didn't feel good or right.

"Laurel, your mother had her reasons."

"Really? She had reasons for not telling me who my father is? Maybe he didn't want me. Maybe he wouldn't have been a part of my life. But a name would have been nice. When everyone else in this tiny, gossipy town was talking about me, knowing things or acting as if they knew, it would have been nice if *I* had known."

"This isn't a bad town," Gladys inserted. "Most of the people in Hope are good people. There are always a few busybodies."

"Yes, I know." Laurel wiped a hand over her face, trying to pull herself together. "What do I do now? I don't want to be the town scandal again."

Gladys reached for her hand. "You were never a scandal and still aren't. Thirty years ago, two young people made a mistake. But *you're* not a mistake. You're my granddaughter. You are your mother's joy. And your father would like to get to know you. He regrets not being a part of your life."

"That's something he should tell me himself. You'll say whatever you need to say to make me feel better. It's your job as a grandmother."

Gladys laughed at that. "I do love you, honey, but I promise, I won't say what makes you feel good. If you need honesty, I'll give it to you."

"Thank you," Laurel said as she scooted off the bed and leaned to kiss her grandmother's cheek. "Is there anything you need me to do while I'm here?"

"Take care of Rose. Make sure if that caseworker calls or comes around that she knows Rose is safe and I'll be home soon. Every time I take a breath, they threaten to take that girl away. She doesn't need to be moved again."

"I'll do what I can," Laurel promised.

"And you'll be nice to my neighbor?" Gladys reached out a hand. "Help me up."

"I doubt I'll see much of him. He doesn't seem to be a social butterfly."

Gladys smiled at that. "No, but Rose has taken it upon herself to drag him out from time to time. Also, Rose likes church. She's involved in the youth group. It gives her something to do with her time aside from school, and it keeps her out of trouble."

"I doubt that."

Gladys laughed. "Well, maybe you're right. But still… it helps."

"Do you still go to Hope Community."

"I do," Gladys confirmed. "Don't get that look on your face. You can't make judgments based on the people and situations from twenty years ago."

"I know."

Something in her face must have given her away because Gladys pointed a finger at her. "You have to go with her."

"I'd rather not, Gran."

"There are always things we'd rather not do. But we do them because it's right. I hadn't planned on taking in a teenager at my age. Yet here I am. We never know what God has in front of us, Laurel, but we can rest assured He has a plan."

A knock on the door ended their conversation.

"Come in," Gladys called in a singsong voice.

Dora stepped through the door, a hand on Rose's shoulder. The girl squirmed out from under the hand and hurried to Laurel's side.

"This young woman brought a kitten into our facility and it frightened one of our residents and then climbed the curtains. She and her kitten need to leave."

"Oh, fine, kick me out." Rose put a hand over the hissing feline in her pocket. "Me and Christmas. Kicked to the curb like yesterday's bad news."

"That is *not* what I'm doing," Dora exclaimed. Her gaze shot to Gladys. "Gladys, I am not responsible for eliminating Christmas from this facility. Just the tree."

"And gifts for residents who have no family," Gladys reminded. "Don't worry about it, Dora, we'll think of something."

Dora nodded, then gave Rose another hard glare. "The child and the kitten need to leave now."

Gladys waved her away. "We understand. I'll say goodbye and they'll go. Thank you, Dora."

Dora gave them one last look that said she clearly didn't trust them and then she left the room.

Gladys climbed onto her bed. "I've always liked Dora. She lives in Grove and she's been the administrator here for years. But this new owner, she's just caved to them."

"Probably out of her control," Laurel offered. "She needs the job and they're calling the shots."

"We'll do something to bring Christmas to the nursing home, Gladys," Rose said with a big smile. "I have ideas."

"I can't wait to hear them! Now, you two head home and feed my animals. I'm going to take a nap."

Laurel gave her grandmother a hug, watched as Rose did the same and then they both left. She didn't know how her quick trip to Hope had changed so much.

Her mother had failed to mention Curt Jackson, a recalcitrant teen, a terrorizing kitten and a reclusive cowboy.

All just in time for Christmas.

Chapter Four

"Can we decorate the tree?" Rose asked as she skipped into the kitchen on Wednesday morning.

Laurel had been in town not even a week but it hadn't taken Rose long to adjust to the new person in the house.

Laurel pulled eggs out of the fridge. "Want to help me make muffins?" Baking was how she and her mom had bonded, also it had given them time to talk during Laurel's difficult teen years. It made sense, in light of that, that Laurel had developed a love for baking. She'd found that it helped her relax. The kitchen was where she found peace.

"Sure, but I only have thirty minutes before the bus gets here. Or you could drive me to school."

"I just might do that. Can you crack eggs and then measure out the milk and melted butter? The recipe is on that card in the stand."

"You're really going to let me help?" Rose tossed her books on the counter.

"That's the general idea when someone says, 'Do you want to help?'"

Rose cracked an egg into a large bowl. Laurel tried to hide her cringe as the girl reached into the bowl to pull out bits of eggshell.

"Here's a spoon. If you get shells in the bowl you can use it."

"No problem, I got them." Rose wiped the shell on a paper towel. "So about the tree?"

"I don't know where the tree is. I'm sure Gladys will put it up when she gets home."

Laurel's smile dissolved. She reached for the cup of melted butter and poured it in with the eggs she'd beaten. "Yeah, I guess. But that will be almost Christmas. And what if I'm gone?"

"You won't be gone." Laurel measured out the baking powder. "Pour in the milk and mix it all together so I can add the dry ingredients."

Rose did as she was told. "What kind of muffins are we making?"

"Pumpkin." Laurel handed her the can. "Scoop that out and add it to the bowl."

"This looks like a lot of muffins."

"I'm going to take some to the nursing home."

Rose's smile reappeared. "You do have a heart."

The teenager hopped onto a stool at the counter and pulled the kitten out of her pocket. Laurel looked up from mixing the dry ingredients in with the wet.

"Kittens do not go on counters," she said as she picked it up. "Have you fed it?"

"It's a she, not an it." Rose plucked the kitten from Laurel's hand. "And yes, I fed her. And I fed the dog, too."

"The stray?"

"It's still a dog and deserves to be fed. But I think the kitten is too young to eat the dry cat food. She cried all night." She grabbed the milk jug and poured milk in a saucer.

Laurel looked up from filling the muffin cups. She studied the kitten and then the girl. Rose's eyes were puffy, her nose red. She thought maybe the kitten hadn't been the only one crying all night. With limited kid and kitten experience, she didn't know if she should say something, ask if she was okay or pretend she didn't notice.

She thought about what her mother would have done in this situation. She should call her mom. They'd had a brief conversation her first night here, very brief. Laurel had asked about Curt Jackson and then she'd been too upset to finish talking to her mother, the person she'd always been able to talk to.

"What do you think is wrong with her?" Laurel asked.

"Misses her mom." She shoved the kitten back in her pocket. "She wants her family."

"She won't fit in your pocket much longer."

"I know, but for now she does and she likes it. I think because it's warm. Anyway, she has to go back to her mother. I don't think she can wait until I get home from school."

"What's your suggestion?"

"You could take her up to the barn."

Laurel slid the muffin tin into the oven and set the timer. "Me? I'm not the one who took her from her mother."

Rose glared.

"All right, I'll take the kitten to her mother." Laurel leaned against the counter. "But I'm sure she's happy with you, too. She knows you love her."

"Don't," Rose warned. "I already have a therapist. I don't need to be analyzed by you."

"Oh." Laurel didn't know what to say.

"Sometimes I miss my mom. She was a bad parent but that doesn't mean I don't love her or that she didn't love me. I can miss her. I learned that from my therapist. I can especially miss her at Christmas, even though she never really did anything Christmassy. I really want to decorate a tree."

Laurel gave Rose a minute to collect herself. She poured

the girl a glass of milk, checked the muffins in the oven and returned to continue the conversation.

"I'll see if I can find the tree. And I'll take the kitten over to her mother in the barn. And I know it isn't easy, missing someone."

She'd never known her dad, but she'd always missed him.

"Yeah, okay." Rose buried her nose in the kitten's soft fur. "Those muffins almost ready? Maybe you could take Cam a couple and ask if he knows where the tree is?"

"Cam?"

"Cameron. You know, the guy that lives in the cottage."

"Yes, I know who he is."

"He might know where the tree is. Maybe if you take him food, you can ask."

"If I see him, I'll ask him."

From the road she heard a car honk. She hurried to the front of the house in time to spot the school bus slowing. She started to yell for Rose but the girl already had her backpack thrown over her shoulder as she was running out the door, waving as she ran down the drive.

"The kitten is on the kitchen floor," Rose yelled back to her. "I'll have muffins for a snack after school."

"I was going to drive you," Laurel called out, but it was too late. She closed the door and then leaned against it. "This can't be my life."

From the kitchen she heard a small mew and then the timer on the stove beeped. She removed the muffins from the oven and picked up the kitten. The tiny gray feline purred and nuzzled against her.

"You do need your mommy, don't you? Let's go see if we can find her." She would take the kitten back and ask about the tree.

As she approached the building, she heard music. She

slowed, taking cautious steps forward. What she was hearing wasn't coming from the radio. The strumming of the guitar was soft and the words of the song muffled. She leaned in closer, trying to catch the words of the song. For several minutes she stood listening. The music grew louder, then boot steps shuffled.

"Are you enjoying the concert?"

She jumped. Cameron Hunter stood in the doorway of the stable, a tall and imposing figure with his black cowboy hat pulled low and a flannel jacket over a dark T-shirt. A guitar hung from the strap around his neck. Her first instinct was to make an excuse or deny that she'd been listening. But, of course, he knew the truth. A person lurking outside a barn was obviously a person up to something.

She said the first thing to pop into her head. "I'm looking for a Christmas tree."

"Out here?" he asked, a half grin tugging at his mouth. He looked around and shrugged. "I think I'd look somewhere else. Unless you're planning to cut one down."

"No, of course not. I promised Rose I would ask. I also had to bring the kitten back to her mother. Have you seen the mama cat?"

"She was lurking in corners. Sound familiar?"

Laurel rolled her eyes at the accusation. "I wasn't lurking, I was listening to your music. You're very good."

"Thank you. And the mother cat is in the far stall with her kittens. I think she'll be glad to see that one. She's been looking for her."

"Yes, Rose realized she took her away from her family too soon."

He motioned her to the end of the barn. "I think Rose wants something of her own. Even if it's just a kitten. Having a pet is a sign of permanence."

Of course, that made perfect sense. She'd been so immersed in her own thoughts, feeling sorry for herself, she hadn't thought about Rose. She might be *Trouble* with a capital *T*, but she was also a child whose mother was missing and her only real stability was an elderly woman in a nursing home.

"She seemed sad this morning," Laurel noted as she walked through the door of the stall to find the mother cat with the rest of the litter.

He paused at that. "I can imagine. She's lost everyone, and even though Gladys isn't going anywhere, I could see that it would worry Rose."

"Do you know where her mother is?" Laurel asked.

"No one knows. Family Services has tried to locate her but she hasn't made contact in six months. She left Rose on a friend's couch and took off, supposedly for California."

"That's tough. Poor Rose."

"Yeah, it is. But Rose is also tough." He leaned on the stall door to watch as the kitten reunited with her mother. The orange, black and white calico immediately curled up with her baby and began to give the gray kitten a good bath.

"Oh, I brought muffins." Laurel handed him the bag she'd carried from the house. "Rose said I'm required to feed you."

"You're not, but thank you." He took the bag and opened it.

She backed away and as she did, he gave her his right side. Did he do it consciously, to make people more at ease? Or was it habit? She started to ask but then didn't. They weren't friends. They were barely acquaintances. She didn't have a right to know his stories. And yet she couldn't walk away.

"I'm going to see my grandmother. I promised to bring her lunch."

His fingers, long and slim, suntanned from time working outside, strummed the guitar. She watched, mesmerized.

"I considered visiting her this afternoon. She made me feel guilty the other day. I should visit more often."

"I'm sure she understands."

"I'll give you a ride if you think you'll be ready by eleven," he continued. The offer took her by surprise.

"Oh, that would be good."

"We can't have you getting lost." He winked and she thought he had no idea how lost he could make a girl feel. It had nothing to do with a malfunctioning GPS or a not-so-helpful teen.

Maybe it was just that he had that unavailable vibe and every girl liked a challenge. Every girl but her. She didn't want to conquer the walls he'd obviously constructed to protect himself. She didn't want to know all of his secrets and heal his brokenness. She would leave that for some romantic soul out there waiting to fix a broken man and call him her own.

Laurel wasn't that person. She was here for a week or so, just long enough to make sure her grandmother was okay.

"I'll be ready to go by eleven," she told him as she walked away, totally unaffected.

At least that's what she told herself.

Cameron had been surprised that Laurel took him up on his offer to give her a ride to Lakeside Manor to visit Gladys. He should have been more surprised with himself for offering. As he stepped out into the hall of the nursing home in order to give Laurel time alone with her grandmother, he realized he'd fallen into Gladys's plans, the ones that ultimately dragged him into her granddaughter's life. He had to give it to her, she was good at meddling.

As he left the room, he heard Laurel telling Gladys that

she couldn't stay in town more than two weeks. She had signed up to start classes in January. She was going to be a teacher. Reinventing herself, Gladys had said, almost approvingly.

He didn't get it. He didn't want to reinvent himself; he just wanted to find a way to live the life he already had. He'd spent the better part of two years figuring it out. He'd spent a lot of that time alone. As Gladys liked to say, "licking his wounds." He couldn't disagree.

A lot had changed in his life. Too much. And it went beyond his injuries. He'd lost his dad. The family ranch had been sold because Cameron and his siblings hadn't wanted to return to the place where they'd spent their childhood years working long hours side by side with their father rather than doing what other kids their age had been doing—movies on Friday nights and swimming on weekends.

The sale of the ranch had given them all the freedom to make their own choices. His choice was to stay in Hope, raise horses and live his life exactly the way he wanted.

He bought a soda from a vending machine and headed back to Gladys's room.

Gladys waved him in, a smile of greeting quick to replace the frown she'd worn when he stepped through the door. If he had to guess, they'd been discussing Curt Jackson. Laurel stood at the window, her back to him. The light cast her in silhouette but didn't hide the fact that she surreptitiously swiped her hand over her cheek.

"Did Laurel ask about your Christmas tree?" he asked. "Rose wants to put up a tree."

"Christmas tree?" Gladys shook her head. "I don't have an artificial tree. I usually buy one in town. Laurel, you'll have to get a tree for Rose to decorate. I think she hasn't had much of a Christmas the past few years. Probably ever, if I had to guess. Get one of the trees that are in planters, so we can replant it after the holidays."

"I'll take Laurel by the feed store," Cameron offered. "We can put the tree in the back of my truck."

Gladys gave him a narrow-eyed look. "Well, now, isn't that nice of you."

"I usually am nice," he reminded. "And it isn't as if Laurel can put a tree in her car, can she?"

"It's just… You usually avoid town like the plague. But since you're being so nice, you can make sure Rose gets to church on Sunday, too."

Cam frowned. "I think I've just been set up."

"It's important to Rose," Gladys insisted. "She's so excited about being in the Christmas program. There are also a couple of programs at school that she will attend. Now you have to make sure you ask because she's so used to not being able to do those things that she'll probably just assume that no one is interested in going or taking her."

"I'll make sure she gets to church and I'll take her to the school programs," Laurel assured her grandmother. "I won't let you down."

Gladys patted her hand. "I know you won't. And now, the two of you should go. I need a nap."

Once they were outside, Laurel turned to him. "You don't have to take me to get a tree."

Walking toward his truck, she was on his left side. He slowed, and with his hands on her arms, he guided her to his right side.

"I like to see the person I'm talking to and I don't like walking with my head constantly turned to the left."

Pink tinged her cheeks. "I'm sorry. I didn't think about that."

"There's no reason you should have. I just thought I'd let you know."

When they reached his truck, he opened the door for her. She looked surprised by the gesture. "Do men in Chicago not open doors for women?" he asked.

"I'm sure they do. I just haven't met any of those men."

"Well, now you've met one." He closed the door, needing that solid piece of metal between them.

He counted to ten, then got in behind the wheel. "I don't mind taking you to get the tree but do you think we should wait till after school and let Rose help pick it out?"

"That sounds great, except I'm starving."

He started his truck. "We can have lunch at the café in Hope."

"You don't have to do that."

He glanced her way before pulling from his parking space. "I don't mind."

"I think you do."

He sighed. "I think you like to argue. This back and forth is making me dizzy."

She laughed. "I guess maybe I do like to argue. But I also don't want you to feel like I'm making you do this."

They drove in silence for several minutes before he responded. "It's okay to be pushed from my comfort zone. When I moved into the cottage at Gladys's, I knew she'd push. It's her nature. She pushes herself and everyone around her."

"Yes, she certainly is a force to be reckoned with. And now you have Rose."

"Capital T," he reminded her. "And she is a force. But so are you."

Surprise flickered through her hazel eyes. "Me? I'm not a force."

He laughed at her. "Oh, you're a force, all right. Kittens, Christmas trees, trips to the nursing home."

"I'm not making you do any of those things," she reminded him.

How well he knew that. The problem was that she didn't have to force him out of his den—he came willingly for her. He used his music to soothe his horses or to gentle an unexpectedly shy or difficult animal. She was his music.

That was probably the most dangerous thought he'd had in a long time.

Chapter Five

When they walked through the door of Holly's Café, all eyes turned in their direction. It was unconscious but she sidled in close to Cameron's side, where it felt safe from prying eyes and questioning gazes. Once she was next to him, she realized she liked how it felt there, at his side. It felt more than safe, it felt strangely right.

A woman with long dark hair and dark eyes hurried their way. "Cameron Hunt, it's been months! What's brought you out for lunch? And who's your friend?"

"Holly, this is Laurel Adams, Gladys's granddaughter."

"Laurel Adams. Oh, my goodness. We went to school together."

Laurel had to think back more than twenty years, to Mrs. Parker's third grade class, then she remembered. Dark-haired, dark-eyed and with a home life less than perfect. The two had been the class misfits—and best friends.

"I do remember!" she said. "It's been a long time, Holly."

"It has. Come on in and I'll give you two my best table." Holly laughed. "As you can see, it's past the lunch-hour rush. The crowd that's here now are all just big gossips taking up space and drinking my coffee."

Cameron had stopped to talk to a group of men at a

big table for ten. One older gentleman, with graying hair, stubbled cheeks and a strong jaw, looked from Cameron to Laurel and back to Cameron. A sly look entered his eyes.

"For a man escorting a pretty woman, you sure look down in the mouth," the man said, a faint tremor in his voice. "I'm guessing this is Gladys's granddaughter, Laurel. I remember her from when she and her mother lived in Hope."

Cameron sighed and pulled her to his right side again. "Laurel, this charming gentleman is Jack West."

Laurel reached for his extended but trembling hand. "Mr. West, it's nice to meet you."

"It's good to have you back in the area. I hope you'll stay awhile." He released her hand. "The two of you should join us. It isn't often we get Cameron to town and I'm curious as to what he has on his mind."

They sat opposite Jack West and introductions were made. Laurel tried to catch the names of all the men at the table. Two were obviously Jack's sons, the others lived and worked on Mercy Ranch.

Holly handed them menus and filled coffee cups. Jack tapped his cup. "And by the way, I heard you call us gossips, Holly," he told the café owner.

She filled his cup, then stirred in a spoon of sugar for him. "You know I was only telling the truth."

Jack West laughed. "I guess it might have been at that. Go ahead and put their order on my tab."

"How's Gladys doing?" Jack asked Laurel.

"Good," she said. "She's scheduled to be out the day after Christmas but I have a feeling she'll try to get home sooner."

During their visit that morning, her grandmother had filled her in on the situation with Rose, and relayed the caseworker's threat to move her to a foster home with a younger couple. Or a group home. But the group home would be in Tulsa or Oklahoma City. Laurel could see how much that threat affected her grandmother and she knew that Rose would be devastated.

"I'm afraid if she isn't out of there by Christmas, she'll have the residents staging a revolt," Cameron added.

Jack grinned at that statement, revealing a charm that he'd probably perfected over the years. "What's going on at the Manor?"

"They won't allow a tree or any other Christmas decorations or celebrations. I think it's just a way to make the place look more profitable, but it definitely hurts the residents who have little enough cheer in their lives."

Jack sat back in his chair and waited as Holly took their orders. She didn't hurry away but instead remained at the side of the table to listen.

"Now that's a real shame," Jack said in a gravelly voice. "I can't imagine we'd let them get away with that. They might not want to provide Christmas but we can figure something out. We all know folks that live there, and some of them don't have any close family or friends in the area. I think we should add Lakeside Manor to the list of people and charities that can be helped by the Christmas at the Ranch event we're planning. Obviously folks from the manor can't attend, but we can make sure donations are taken to them."

The door to the café opened. Jack West shot a quick look at the person entering, then he shifted his concerned gaze to Laurel. He cleared his throat.

Laurel moved in her chair so that she could see who had caught his attention. Her breath caught as Curt Jackson stopped in the middle of the café. So, not everyone in Hope was unaware of who her father was. Jack West obviously knew.

"I need to go," she said, scooting her chair back from the table. "I'm sorry."

"What?" Cameron had just picked up his glass of sweet tea. "Didn't we just order lunch?"

Jack jerked his head toward the door, a not-so-subtle gesture that made Laurel cringe. Cameron turned around to see who'd just entered.

"You stay and eat. I'll go." Laurel grabbed her purse and headed for the door. She wasn't surprised when Curt Jackson reached for her. She evaded the gesture and hurried for the door.

"Just give me a minute," he called out as he followed her out the door.

"I don't think you deserve a minute," she told him.

He followed her down the sidewalk. At the corner they both stopped. That's when she turned to face him. He was close to fifty, or so she guessed. His red hair had more brown in it and his face was weathered and deeply lined.

"Laurel, I would have married your mother but I didn't know about you until after I was married."

She waited, needing more than that. She wanted him to say something that mattered but didn't know what.

He tugged down on the brim of his cowboy hat and shifted his gaze to the lake.

"I was a coward," he finally said. "It was easier to send your mother the money to start over in Chicago than to explain to my wife, Marla, that I had a daughter living in Hope. I eventually told her and she said she'd always known. Someone here told her. But again, we just didn't communicate."

"That's it? Lack of communication is why I grew up not knowing my father's name?"

He looked sad. He looked sorry. And she didn't know

what to feel, other than anger and loss. She didn't feel much like forgiveness right now.

"At least now I know your name and I know who I look like." Questions she'd had her entire life finally answered.

She'd actually prayed for this. She told herself she should be thankful but it was hard to do after so many years of feeling ignored.

Somewhere in the distance a church bell rang. She closed her eyes as the tones filled the quiet country afternoon.

"Have you talked to my mother?" she asked him.

"I have." He glanced in the direction of the café. The door had opened and Jack West was exiting with the help of his sons. Curt nodded a greeting. "She thought we would meet eventually, but not this way. I planned on having Gladys set up a time."

"Surprise."

He grimaced. "I know we should have done this differently, but I am so glad to finally meet you, Laurel. I hope we can take some time to get to know one another."

"Do I have siblings?" She'd always wondered about that.

"No." He shrugged. "Marla and I couldn't have children."

"I see."

The bell on the café door jangled again. Cameron exited with a to-go bag in his hand.

"I have to go," she told the man standing in front of her. Her father. A stranger. She let her gaze drop to his hands. Her hands.

"Can we set a time to talk?" he asked.

She nodded but she wasn't ready. Not yet. "Soon."

He touched her shoulder and, with a nod, walked down the sidewalk, leaving her alone. A moment later Cameron joined her, his already familiar cologne a steady presence.

He stood next to her, his gaze on the lake less than half a mile away.

"Well, that went well." She smiled up at him. "Thank you for bringing my food."

"You said you were hungry."

"Yes, thanks." She took the bag from him.

Together they walked toward his truck. "You okay?"

"I'm fine. I mean, why wouldn't I be? I just met my father."

"Curt Jackson. He's a decent man."

"Is he?" She thought about that, about all of the things she might learn about the man who was her father.

"Let's walk a bit. It's warm today and taking a walk always helps me clear my head." He made the offer and started to walk, not waiting for her reply.

"You have other things to do. I've dragged you to see Gladys, forced you to get lunch with me…"

"I can assure you, you haven't forced me to do anything. I'm fully capable of saying no when I choose to."

They walked side by side down the sidewalk to a park located across the street from the Hope Community Church, the church she'd attended as a child. It looked the same. The white siding, the tall bell tower, a side wing that had been added in the seventies. A nativity had been set up in the front of the church.

The entire town had been decorated for Christmas, it seemed. Lights hung from electric poles. The stores were layered in lights, garland and wreaths. Trees sparkled in storefronts. She loved that the little town had come back to life with the help of Jack West and people willing to start fresh with new stores.

Starting over. Something she would soon be doing. With the demise of her bakery, she knew it was time to go in a new direction. Or perhaps return to her previous plan. She'd always wanted to teach but she'd pushed aside that career goal when she'd started a catering business with a friend, and then had started her bakery.

She sat on a bench facing the church. Cameron sat next to her. A cool breeze blew but the sun was warm on them. It did feel good to be outside.

"I didn't enjoy church when I was a kid," she admitted. "I knew people judged my mother. I heard whispers. People would talk about my red hair. I never heard them mention Curt Jackson, but they all must have known. Or suspected."

"It's a small town. People talk. You can't run from that."

She gave him a sideways glance because she wondered if he hadn't been doing his own share of running.

"No, you can't outrun the past or the gossip," she agreed. "What about you, Cameron? Are you running?"

Surprise registered on his expression. He hadn't expected the question. She hadn't expected to ask him something so personal. That wasn't who she was, delving into the lives of people who were little more than strangers. She'd always had a live-and-let-live policy. But sitting here with him she realized it was more than average curiosity that caused her to ask the question.

She found herself truly wanting to know him.

Cameron was taken by surprise, by the question, by the woman sitting next to him. He watched as she buttoned her jacket, maybe to avoid looking at him. The wind suddenly picked up and clouds began to cover up the blue sky above them. In the distance he could hear Christmas carols playing over one of the speakers hooked up to light poles on the main street.

The woman sitting next to him looked beat up. Emotionally. She'd picked at the salad she'd ordered and was now staring at the church across the street from the park.

"We all have things we're trying to run from," he admitted. "A law degree was my way of escaping the family ranch, church on Sundays and my father, with all of his rules. Church had even more rules. I guess it made sense that I considered a degree in law. Law follows rules. But now I regret running. I regret the years I lost with my dad."

"I think we all have regrets. I shouldn't have avoided my grandmother. I think that's the good thing that has come out of this trip. I can rebuild my relationship with her."

"And meeting your dad?"

"I'm not sure about that yet." Her voice took on a faraway tone and she slipped the takeout container back into the bag. "Thank you for sitting here with me."

The side door of the church opened and the pastor's wife walked out, carrying a box. She saw them and waved, then headed for the sign at the edge of the lawn.

"Sermons on a sign," Laurel said.

"Yes, I guess they are. Sixty-second sermons for people driving by. Get their attention, make them think and maybe they'll show up on Sunday morning."

"Does it work that way?"

"Maybe."

The words began to take shape on the sign. "'Faith is more than a building or church attendance. It's a way of life.'"

"That's a good one."

Cameron glanced at the woman sitting next to him. "Sermon on a sign."

"Yes. I have some good memories in that little church. Willa Mae Wilkins taught our Sunday school. It wasn't all bad. I think people just don't stop to consider how their words can wound the heart of a child. Of anyone, really."

"No, sometimes they don't."

She shivered and hugged her arms around herself. He

wondered if it was the memories or the cool air blowing in from the north.

She grinned at him. "My favorite sermon on a sign was 'Love one another is a way of life, not a slogan on a shirt.'"

"I think I've seen it on this sign." He considered his next words carefully. "And I've seen it lived in this church."

"Okay."

"I'm not lecturing, just saying, perspective and time change things. Change people."

"Yes, they do. And I'm not walking on water. I know I should have been here more often to visit my grandmother." She studied the sign, then smiled up at him, her hazel eyes misty. "Let's change the subject. Something not so deep or emotional."

"We could go pick Rose up at school, then get ourselves a Christmas tree," Cameron suggested. He stood and held out his hand. She took it and he pulled her to her feet. But he didn't let go of her hand.

As he stood there staring down at her, he found himself reluctant to let go. She looked up, her expression registering the same surprise he felt. He couldn't say that he'd ever felt this way, just holding a woman's hand. It was as if the wind was suddenly calm.

He'd been spending too much time alone. That was the only explanation he could come up with. Alone there were no questions, no one asking how he was doing. No curious souls asking him what had happened to him. He didn't have to fear that if he heard a loud noise, he'd want to run for cover and drag everyone in the vicinity to safety with him.

And, yes, it had happened, more than once.

He'd embraced his solitary existence. But the solitary life was cracking all around him, as if he was standing on a frozen lake. The hand-holding had made it evident he wasn't alone. The woman staring up at him didn't do so with a look of fear or disgust. She looked at him the way few people had done since the explosion. She looked at him as if he was still whole.

And that made him feel whole.

Her hand squeezed his, bringing him out of his thoughts. She smiled. "Are you okay?"

She wouldn't want the real answer. "I'm good," he answered.

"We could do that. We could pick Rose up and go pick out a tree. Do you think she's ever done anything like that?"

"Probably not. She told us she's looking forward to Christmas and having a real family. She worries a lot that caseworkers will move her."

"My grandmother mentioned that today. She said the caseworker will visit the house tomorrow. If they don't feel comfortable with Rose remaining with me until Gladys gets home, they'll move her to a foster home."

"As much as she's always in my business, I don't want her gone."

"No, I'm sure you don't." She took a breath, as if fortifying herself. She withdrew her hand. "Okay, let's go get her."

They pulled up to the school and both of them got out and walked up to the front doors. He pushed the button and a moment later they were buzzed in. The secretary smiled when they walked through the door.

"Hello, Cam." She pushed a sign-out sheet across her desk. "Here to get Rose?"

"Is it okay if we take her a few minutes early?" he asked.

"I think so. Are you taking her to see Gladys?"

He signed the sheet. "No, we're taking her to pick out a Christmas tree."

"Perfect. I'll call her down."

When Rose saw them, she rushed at them both, hugging them in turns. "What are you doing here?" And then her face fell. "Is Gladys okay?"

"Gladys is fine," Laurel assured the girl. "We're here to take you tree shopping."

"A real tree?" she asked. She was already heading to the door, talking nonstop.

"This is just like having a real family. I've watched kids with real families. Their parents show up for school programs. No one ever showed up for my school stuff until Gladys. And then she got hurt. But going to get a tree together is like total family. Can we get hot chocolate at the store?"

Cameron groaned. "Can you take a breath and slow down? My head is spinning with all of your plans."

She smiled and took a deep breath.

In blessed silence they drove the short distance to the feed store, where a portable round pen had been set up and inside it were a variety of evergreen trees, some in tubs of dirt to allow for replanting after Christmas.

The silence didn't last. As they parked, Rose erupted again.

"Wow, look at all of those trees! Could we make homemade decorations? And I had an idea. Sunday at church I'm going to see if we can paint Christmas trees on paper. We can make dozens and take them to the nursing home. Everyone who wants one can have one for their room."

Laurel smiled at Cameron over the top of Rose's head. Her arms went around the girl, drawing her close. "I can definitely help with decorations. And the paper trees are a great idea."

"You'll be at church, too—you could help," Rose added.

Cameron watched as Laurel began to respond, probably

to reject the idea, but Rose was already making a beeline for the trees. Laurel shook her head.

"How did that happen?" she asked as Cameron joined her.

"I warned you. *Trouble* with a capital *T.* You'll get sucked in faster than you can say her name."

"I think I'm learning that."

He found himself smiling as he watched Rose slip between trees, awestruck and happy. "She isn't all bad."

"No, she isn't," Laurel said in a thoughtful tone. "She makes me thankful for my childhood. I have so many wonderful holiday memories. Not just Christmas, but throughout the years. Those memories should be treasured."

He leaned his arms on the top rail of the round pen. "I've ignored Christmas for the past few years. It was easier to be alone than to face everything I've lost. But you can't ignore Christmas with someone like Rose around. She's reminded me of what it means to share this holiday, to feel the love of family and friends."

"Our holidays have been quiet. There were a few years when my grandmother visited us in Chicago, but other than that, it's been my mom and me. My mom is a nurse so her schedule made it difficult to do much."

"I found the tree," Rose called out. "It's perfect."

"Perfect?" Laurel saw the huge tree Rose was referring to and shot Cameron a look, silently asking him to intervene. No way would he tell Rose she couldn't have the mammoth tree she'd picked.

"That's a beauty," he called out. Laurel gave him a death glare that only made him laugh.

"It won't fit in the house," she insisted.

Cameron remained leaning on the pen, watching as Laurel, with her red hair coming free of the bun she'd secured it in, walked around the tree. Her cheeks were red from the cold air and her lips were shiny from the gloss she'd applied. She looked like Christmas. She was tinsel, twinkling lights and laughter.

And he couldn't stop himself from thinking about how much he didn't want her to leave.

Chapter Six

Laurel popped popcorn while Rose put a needle and thread through cranberries. Rose had the decorations all planned out. Paper snowflakes, popcorn balls, cranberry garlands and a few ornaments they'd found hidden in a closet. Mostly homemade or ornaments Laurel's mother had sent to Gladys over the years.

Rose had told her they were going to turn the house into Christmas.

"What's for dinner?" Rose asked as she threaded cranberries.

"Potato soup." Laurel was glad for the reminder. She reached under the cabinet for the potatoes she'd bought the previous day. "And, of course, homemade hot cocoa."

"Homemade?" Rose's gaze shot up for a brief moment. "Like not out of a package?"

"Not out of a package."

"Whoa, that's awesome. Did you invite Cam to come over?"

Laurel poured the popcorn into a bowl. "I did but I don't think he's coming down."

"Hmm, okay." Rose slid another cranberry onto the string. "Are you staying until Christmas?"

"No, probably not. I have to move out of my apartment by the end of the month. And my mom is going to try to come down here for a few days."

Rose was silent. Laurel took a handful of popcorn from the bowl, not caring that it wasn't salted or buttered. She chewed on a few kernels as she watched the teenager struggle to continue smiling.

"Rose?"

Rose swiped at a tear rolling down her cheek and shook her head. "Don't be all nice and sympathetic. It doesn't matter."

"What doesn't matter?"

"Don't you understand? If you leave town, and Gladys isn't here, the caseworker will move me to a foster home. Not that it matters to you, because you don't really know me and I guess you don't even know your grandmother. But I know her, and I don't want to leave."

"Rose, I'll do my best to make sure they don't take you. I know my grandmother doesn't want them to take you."

"But if you stay…"

"I can't stay." Laurel felt the words were less than convincing. The look Rose gave her confirmed her suspicions. "I have to get a job. I have college classes. My life isn't here in Hope."

"I guess not." Rose shrugged it off. "It's fine. People leave."

"We have two weeks until Christmas. I won't leave for a week or so. That gives us time to figure something out."

"Yeah, okay." Laurel looked at the bright red berry in her hand. "They aren't real berries, are they?"

"No, I don't think so. I'm not sure, though."

Rose eyed the fruit, then smiled up at Laurel. "Can you eat them raw?"

"I guess you can but I wouldn't if I were you."

"Dare me to try it?"

Laurel shook her head. "No, I don't."

Rose popped the cranberry in her mouth and immediately winced. But she didn't spit it out. She chewed and chewed and finally swallowed.

"Oh, wow. That was horrible. Who eats those things?"

"People generally cook them with a lot of sugar before they eat them."

Rose reached for her glass of water. "That's just wrong."

Laurel couldn't help but laugh. "Yeah, well, if I was you, I'd eat the muffins I made this morning. It'll get the taste out of your mouth."

"That sounds good." But then she popped another cranberry in her mouth.

"Why?" Laurel asked.

"Because I just had to. I don't know why. They were there, they're bright red, they're shiny. Try one." She gave Laurel one.

"I don't think I want to." She looked at the shiny berry in her hand. Were they berries?

A knock on the door diverted Laurel's attention. "I'll get that."

She headed for the door, and for some crazy reason she put the cranberry in her mouth. She opened the door as she chewed, her eyes watering as the sour tanginess filled her mouth.

Cameron stepped inside, holding up a bag. "I brought pinecones for decorations."

His narrow-eyed gaze was on her as he removed his hat and stuck it on the hook next to the door. He faced her again, and she could only see him. The man. Not the scars on his face. Not the growl that he hid behind. She saw a man who was worth knowing. A man who cared that a recalcitrant teen had a merry Christmas.

"We're tasting cranberries," Rose called out from the kitchen as the two adults stood staring at one another. "Want one?"

"Uncooked?" Cameron looked to her for an answer. She nodded.

"Uncooked." Laurel headed for the kitchen and the popcorn. "I didn't mean to. I had it in my hand and suddenly it was in my mouth. At least I didn't eat two of them."

Rose spluttered a bit. "I had to. I mean, it was just there and then I couldn't decide if I liked it or not. It's like I didn't like it but in a weird way, I did."

"I brought ingredients to make my secret-recipe hot cocoa." He set a bag on the counter. "I happen to make the best."

"Marshmallows?" Rose asked.

"It's so good, you don't need marshmallows, but if you must," he told her.

Laurel watched as he made himself at home in Gladys's kitchen, pulling a pan from the cabinet and then pouring in the ingredients. Cocoa, sugar, cinnamon, real vanilla and milk with a drop of cream added for extra richness. The aroma was wonderful. She opened the container with the muffins she'd made that morning.

"I don't have cookies, but we have these." She set three out on plates. "Much better than raw cranberries."

He half grinned as he leaned a hip against the counter. "I'm going to take your word on that and stick to the muffins."

"This is the best time ever." Rose grabbed a muffin and went back to work. "I used to make up things like this. When kids at school would talk about what they were doing for Christmas, I'd pretend my mom and I were going shopping and making candy." She looked up from the string of fruit. "Do you make candy?"

Laurel had to swallow the lump in her throat before she could answer. "I do make candy. Do you want to make fudge or toffee?"

"Both," Rose said. But then her expression fell. "Will we have time? I mean, before you leave."

"We can make it tonight." Laurel avoided eye contact with Cameron because she didn't want to see the disappointment in his expression. Not that she thought he would be disappointed, at least not for himself. He'd be disappointed for Rose.

"We could make candy for the nursing home," Rose responded. "We have to save Christmas for those people. It isn't fair that they might not have anything."

The teen concentrated on pushing the needle through more cranberries, but her expression was about more than the residents of Lakeside Manor. Cameron turned the flame under the pan of hot chocolate down to simmer. He touched Laurel's shoulder as he left the room, leaving them alone.

Laurel realized that she knew very little about children. And she especially didn't know about teenagers. But she did remember how she'd felt as a teen, being the girl who didn't have a father. In her imagination he was sometimes a soldier, sometimes a doctor, maybe a cowboy. In her imagination he'd always been a perfect hero, not a real-life man.

Real-life men were sometimes flawed, sometimes scarred. But they were real and worth knowing.

The situation before her was complex. A girl who wanted a family, who feared being cut off from a life she'd just started to embrace, and the overwhelming fact that without intervention she might have to go away.

"Rose, do you believe in God?"

Rose looked up, her eyes shimmering with unshed tears. "Of course I do. I mean, I had God when I didn't have anyone else."

Laurel felt the air go out of her. When had she ever had such a clearly defined view of faith? She'd been trying to find words to help a child, but the child had all the answers.

"Then we have to trust Him, don't we? Trust that God has a plan, that His ways are higher than our ways and the path He has for us is there, even if we can't see it. Yet."

"What if His plan is for me to leave here?" Rose swallowed. "Or what if the caseworkers aren't listening to God?"

"First, if He has a different plan, we trust it is the best plan. Second, if they aren't listening, we pray that they will listen."

Rose absently reached for another raw cranberry. "They're starting to grow on me."

Laurel laughed. "I could say the same about you."

She heard Cameron's booted steps, and when he entered the kitchen, she had a moment of hesitation. It felt like her heart briefly took a rest and waited for her to catch up. She knew it was attraction but she greatly admired this quiet man, as well.

She would miss the two of them when she left Hope.

Cameron poured hot cocoa in three cups and watched as Laurel showed Rose how to measure the ingredients for fudge. They'd made a pan of peanut-butter fudge and this would be the first pan of chocolate.

"Okay, your turn to stir." Laurel removed her apron.

It took him a moment to understand what she meant but it became obviously clear as she lifted the apron and gave him a look, one ginger eyebrow arched and her lips pursed.

"What?" he asked.

"Lean down so I can help you put this on. If you don't hurry, that fudge will burn and my hot cocoa won't be hot."

"Come on, cowboy, time to make some fudge."

He leaned just a little and he wished he'd just stayed

home. This close to her, she was Christmas. She smelled like cocoa, evergreen and cinnamon. For the past few years he'd convinced himself this couldn't happen—this attraction, this longing to spend more time with someone. And yet here it was, and, of course, it would be with this woman, the one determined to do her time in Hope like it was a prison sentence.

She stilled, her hands holding the apron above him. Her breath caught and she blinked a few times. And then she dropped the apron over his head and backed away.

"Turn around and I'll tie it for you." She said it quietly.

He turned and she quickly tied the apron at his waist.

"What do I do now?" he asked, and the question was loaded. It was about the fudge, about her, about this situation he'd found himself in.

"I've finished cutting the fudge that's cool," Rose said. She stared at the two of them, half amused. "I'm going to feed my dog, then start decorating the tree."

"The stray," Cameron and Laurel said in unison.

"Try to deal with this before I return. Just FYI, I'm a child and I don't like PDA," Rose said pointedly.

"There's not going to be any PDA," Laurel said with a determined tone.

"Right." Rose rolled her eyes and took off.

"She's hilarious," Laurel said as she melted butter in a saucepan.

Cameron glanced down at her. She stood next to him at the stove. It was a unique experience. He'd never shared a kitchen with a woman. They were surrounded by the scent of chocolate, sugar and butter. From the living room, Christmas carols were playing and Rose began to sing along. "Deck the Halls," very off-key.

"I did think about kissing you," he admitted. "But then I realized we're chaperoning a thirteen-year-old."

"Plus, I'm leaving soon," she said softly, glancing up at him. "Where did I put the sugar?"

"Right in front of you," he responded, finding humor in the fact that she was disconcerted by what he'd said. "I was a geek in school."

"What?"

He checked the thermometer in the pan. "What temperature?"

She looked at the timer. "In one minute add the chocolate, marshmallow and vanilla. And explain yourself."

"Tall, skinny, glasses. My nose was too big for my face. I liked striped shirts and cowboy boots. I studied a lot. Not a chick magnet. The one girl I dated in college, the one who said she would marry me, broke it off when I returned from Afghanistan and claimed I wasn't the man she'd known."

"I'm not sure what to say."

"I just wanted you to know… I'm not the man who spends his time hitting on women. I'm not arrogant. I'm not sure of myself. I've had to work really hard to get to the point that I can even go to town, to church."

"I'm sorry."

He stirred ingredients into the saucepan. "I don't need apologies, I'm just explaining a fact. If a car backfires, I might grab you and push you against a wall."

"I'm not made of glass—I'll survive."

"I know." He considered to stir the fudge. "I want to kiss you. I want to see if you really taste like Christmas. Because that's what I imagine. More than that, I want to see if there is something between us that should be explored further."

"Explored?"

He'd reduced her to one-word sentences. He had to put a stop to that. He reached for her hand. She didn't argue, so he pulled her close and moved his other hand to her back. Cameron lowered his head and touched his lips to hers. He moved his hand to her neck and felt her sigh beneath his touch. She kissed him back. It was like a gift. A gift a man should cherish, one he wouldn't want to give back or exchange.

She touched his shoulder and then his face. The left side of his face. Her fingers traced the scars and he allowed it.

"Gross!" Rose yelled from the entrance between the dining room and living room. "Incoming impressionable child."

Laurel gave a shaky laugh and pulled away.

Cameron reached over to turn down the stove. "It's boiling."

She returned her attention to the toffee and gasped. "I think it's too late. I shouldn't have let it get this hot."

Rose slid into the kitchen on stocking feet. She watched as Laurel tried to save the candy, stirring quickly and then pouring it onto the buttered pan.

"If you're done, can we decorate the tree now?"

"Sure thing," Cameron said.

Anything to get his mind off the woman at his side. He needed to refocus and remember that she was from a world completely removed from his. A world she would return to.

Soon.

Chapter Seven

Rose's caseworker showed up at ten o'clock Thursday morning. She was Laurel's age with dark hair pulled back in a ponytail and a friendly smile. She wasn't the enemy, Laurel realized. She was a woman who cared about Rose and wanted to make sure she was safe.

She introduced herself as Carlie and entered the house, taking in the Christmas tree they'd finished decorating the previous evening, as well as the multitude of paper snowflakes hanging from curtain rods, cabinet knobs and anywhere else that Rose deemed necessary. There were also a good dozen for the residents of Lakeside Manor.

"It looks like you've been decorating for Christmas," Carlie said as she took a seat at the kitchen island. "You wouldn't have coffee, would you? Gladys always has coffee."

"Yes, of course." Laurel grabbed a cup and filled it for her.

"Thank you," she sighed as she inhaled the aroma. "I had a call at five this morning. This job is never easy and some of it is downright hard. But Rose, she's going to be our success story, right?"

"I hope she is. She loves being here with Gladys. And Gladys loves her."

"Gladys is your grandmother, correct?" Carlie pulled out a laptop. "We have the paperwork she had you fill out."

"Yes, she is my grandmother and yes, I filled out paperwork and left it with her."

"You know we have concerns. Her age is a strike against her."

"Gladys is more fit than a lot of younger people I know," Laurel said.

"You don't have to tell me," Carlie agreed. "I know, I've met her. I'm just saying, there are some people who worry. I say, let's worry when there's something to really worry about. I do need to do a background check on you. I mean, we ran a quick one through the local police, but we'll have to do one through the state."

"I don't mind. But I'm only going to be here for another week or so."

"Yeah, I get that. But rules are rules." She pulled a paper out of her file. "It's pretty simple and if you can do it now, I'll take it in. We will also have to get your fingerprints. You'll need to go to Grove for that."

"But I'm only going to—"

Carlie waved her hand. "Yeah, yeah, but you're caring for one of our kids and we take their safety seriously. I get it, you're a nice person, but I am responsible for her welfare."

"So am I." Laurel blinked as she said the words. "Okay, just make a list of what I need to do."

Carlie grinned. "Thank you."

"Is there any chance her mom is coming back?" Laurel asked.

The caseworker shook her head. "I doubt it. She's been doing this to Rose for thirteen years. She dumps the kid with a friend or family and takes off. We're going to make sure it doesn't happen again. And as far as I know, her mom is in jail in California."

"Rose doesn't know that?"

"No. I just found out a few days ago."

Laurel poured herself a cup of coffee. "Should I tell her?"

"I think so. No matter what, these kids love their parents. They fantasize about the perfect reunion, where the parent comes back clean and sober, ready to be the mom they always imagined. Who knows, maybe someday Tarin will grow up and be that mom. For now, she isn't able. But Rose is safe and loved and she's got a home. A real home for the first time in her life."

Laurel got it. She herself had felt safe here as a child. Rose was just now figuring out what it meant to be safe.

"So, about Christmas. I have gifts for her. I mean, you all can do what you want for her. She'll love everything you do, including all of this decorating. But I have to warn you, they really are considering moving her to a home with younger foster parents."

"They can't do that." Laurel felt herself go cold at the thought. "Why would they do that when she's safe here and loved? You just said—"

Again Carlie stopped her. "I said what I think. But I'm not in charge. I mean, I am. I'm her caseworker, but I have people I answer to. Those people will make the final decision. We have a court date in January."

"Is there a way we can convince them to leave her here with Gladys?" Laurel asked.

Carlie shrugged. "I'm not sure. Gladys injuring herself and having to spend time in the hospital and nursing home haven't been the best thing for the case. I know Kylie West and Dr. West took great care of Rose, but we can't have her shifted here and there every time Gladys has a health crisis."

"It wasn't a health crisis, it was a broken shoulder."

"From falling off a half-broke horse," Carlie said with a bit of admiration.

"Right." Laurel sat down next to the caseworker.

"You can't stay? I mean, obviously you have a job in Chicago—"

"I don't," Laurel admitted. "But I'm going back to college."

"Of course. It's too much to ask someone to change their whole life, move hundreds of miles, start over."

"Yes, it's a lot."

Carlie shuffled papers, then dropped them in her briefcase. "Well, I have to go. I'll get all of this done and send you the address for getting your fingerprints taken care of. And I'm leaving a book for you to study, just in case something changes."

"Thanks, I'll take a look."

Laurel walked Carlie to the door, and then she stood looking at the book in her hands. *The Foster Parent Handbook*. Her cell phone rang and she rushed back in to answer it.

"Hey, Mom," she answered.

"Laurel, I tried to call last night. Is everything okay?"

"It's good. The caseworker just left."

"How did that go?"

"There's a January court date and supervisors who don't think Gran is the best candidate for raising a thirteen-year-old. I'm not sure how she or Rose would handle it if they moved Rose."

"No, I can't imagine. We'll have to pray they don't make that decision. But how are you doing? I know this has all been more than you expected."

Laurel thought about that. "Definitely more than I expected, but it isn't terrible. Rose is funny and we're doing fine together."

"And that handsome caretaker of Mom's?"

"Not a caretaker. He's building a house on the property next to hers and renting her cottage and barns until his place is finished."

"I see."

"Nothing to see," Laurel responded. She took a breath to address the elephant in the room. "Mom, we have to discuss Curt Jackson."

"I know we do. I'm sorry."

"Of course you are, but this is a whole lifetime of secrets you've kept from me. I'm angry. I'm hurt. I feel robbed."

"Those feelings are all understandable. I made a really poor choice, keeping this from you. I hope you'll forgive us both. I hope you can find your way to having a relationship with your father."

"I think it's a little too soon to call him that. I feel like that title has to be earned. It's more than just DNA."

"I want us to be able to sit down and discuss this. After Christmas."

"Yes, I'll be home and we can talk." Laurel held the phone for a moment, unsure of what else she could say. "I need to go."

"Laurel, I love you."

"Love you, too." She meant it, but sometimes love hurt.

Laurel glanced out the kitchen window and saw Cameron walking into the barn. She slid her phone in her pocket, grabbed a jacket and headed that way.

The filly wobbled next to her mother, but then she noticed him and took a hesitant step, watching him. She was perfect. She would eventually be a deep red, the same as her sire. The black of her mane and tail would deepen. She flagged that black tail and took a prancing step forward, already trying to show her pride.

"She's beautiful," the voice from behind him said. He turned, smiling at the woman who approached, slowly, as if afraid to frighten the horse.

"Just born this morning. Mama and I were up early this morning, playing some music and watching the sun come up together and then this girl made her appearance." He felt all sentimental, maybe even a little teary. It wouldn't do a lot for his reputation as a cowboy if he cried over the birth of a foal.

But Laurel had tears in her eyes as she watched the baby nuzzle against her mother. He'd let her be the emotional one.

The surprise was when she stepped close to the fence, on his right side, and put her arm around him. He froze as she leaned close, as if they'd been friends forever and not merely days. Who was this woman who'd come into his life, taking up space in a way he hadn't expected?

He should pull away from her, because that's what his sensible self would have done a week or two ago, back when he was still convinced he enjoyed his solitary life here on the hill. Instead he folded his arm over her back to hold her there next to him. They stood like that, watching the mare and foal, for some time.

"You okay?" he asked after they'd been there for several minutes.

She shook her head. "I just spoke with my mother about Curt Jackson. And worse, I don't know what to do for Rose. The caseworker, Carlie, told me they might send her to a foster home."

"I've worried about that. Gladys isn't healthy, Laurel. I know she looks healthy. I know she's active. But the truth is, she's eighty years old and chasing after a thirteen-year-old wears her out."

"I know that. I'm just not sure what to do about it. Rose loves my grandmother and she deserves to have this home."

"I agree."

"This is one of those moments when people say, 'I'll pray.' It's what they say when facing something difficult. But this situation really needs prayer. I know in my heart that God has a plan but I don't know what it is."

She moved out from his embrace and looked up at him. "And you, you've complicated my life. I don't want to get attached to you and then find that it was just Christmas, twinkling lights, paper snowflakes and hot cocoa. Temporary things. All sweet and nice but then we pack them away for the rest of the year."

"Because you're leaving and I like solitude." He got it, he really did.

"Exactly." She cupped his cheek with her gloved hand. "But I do like you, Cameron. If my world wasn't in Chicago…"

"I know." He cleared his throat, needing to find new solid ground to stand on.

They walked back to Gladys's house together but he stopped at the back door. It seemed the right thing to do. She stood on the steps, the breeze lifting the curls she seemed to try so hard to control.

She leaned in to kiss his cheek. "Thank you."

She hurried through the door, and he stood there for a long few minutes, wondering about God and His plans. Because nowhere in his prayers for healing had he thought about Gladys, Rose or Laurel. But now, even if he didn't want to admit it, he felt a lot more like the person he used to be.

Was that because of Laurel?

Chapter Eight

Sunday afternoon, with just over a week until Christmas, Laurel accompanied the youth group from Hope Community Church, as well as a group of adults, to Lakeside Manor nursing home. They had spent the morning putting together small bags of fudge for residents who were allowed sugar, and bags of nuts and fruits for those who weren't. The kids had created artwork to be hung on the walls of the residents' rooms. They'd brought an assortment of painted trees, manger scenes and bible verses. The folks planning Christmas at the Ranch, an event at Mercy Ranch, had donated socks, shirts, nightgowns and other small gifts.

As they entered the facility, Dora came out of her office.

"You thought I wouldn't be here today?" she asked as she surveyed the group of teens waiting for Isaac West and his wife, Rebecca, the youth leaders from Hope Community Church. The couple hadn't shown up yet.

"We brought you some Christmas cheer, Dora." Rose handed over a plate of fudge with a big smile. "These kids have been hard at work preparing Christmas gifts for the residents. We won't bother anyone who doesn't want to be bothered, but we did want to do something for people who have lived their lives, worked hard, served their country and community."

Laurel felt her heart melt just a little. And the administrator's eyes shimmered with tears.

Dora stood there for a long moment, all serious professionalism. Laurel watched in wonder as the other woman seemed to thaw before her eyes. A smile hovered on her lips and she nodded.

"Bless you all," she said. "This is so kind. I'll have our staff bring the residents out to the activity hall, the ones who are able. And if a few of you would like to visit those people who can't leave their rooms, I think that would be nice."

Rose stepped forward and hugged the woman. "Thank you."

"No, thank you. Now come on, let's have an early Christmas."

"I'm going to get my grandmother," Laurel told Rose as the group headed for the activity room.

"You go on," Rose said with an air of authority beyond her years. "We've got this handled."

Laurel watched as the youth group marched down the hall.

She met Gladys coming out of her room.

"What in the world is going on?" Gladys asked, looking less than steady on her feet. Laurel's grandmother reached for the door to steady herself.

"Gran, are you okay?" Laurel reached for her grandmother's hand.

"I'm just fine. I woke up from a nap and heard a ruckus in the hall."

"That would be Rose and the youth group from the church."

"Well, now, this is a lovely surprise. That girl keeps me young."

They were moving slowly in the direction of the main hall when they heard the beginning of "Silent Night." They rounded the corner to see teens lined up down the hall, all singing. The song drifted sweetly through the home.

Gladys stopped, pulling Laurel to a stop next to her. They watched as the teens finished singing and then they all moved together down the center of the hall, in an orchestrated move. As they walked they began to sing "Joy to the World."

More residents came out of their rooms to listen. Laurel watched as some of the older people sang along, and a few wiped tears from their cheeks. She was pretty moved herself. This was the faith of her childhood, put on a shelf and unused for so many years. It sparked inside her, the feeling of warmth spreading as she watched the display of love the teens had for these people.

"God is good," Gladys said softly. "Being here has been tough but some good things came of it. This, for instance. And bringing you home."

Laurel didn't know what to say, but she didn't have time to dwell on it. As she scanned the crowd, listening to the kids sing, she saw him. Curt Jackson stood at the end of the hall, and when she made eye contact, he smiled. All at once she felt cold. She felt hurt all over again.

"You have to forgive," Gladys said, squeezing Laurel's hand. "I know it isn't easy. But you have parents who made mistakes. Forgive them both."

She was silent, standing there watching as the song ended and the teens from the youth group were enveloped in hugs and kisses by the residents and the staff.

Curt Jackson moved through the crowd, heading her way. She knew that he meant to talk to her. She searched the crowd, seeking Cameron. She shook her head at that realization. He wasn't her safety net.

Cameron gaze locked with hers and he gave a slight incline of his head, barely a nod, and smiled.

"Hmm, interesting," Gladys whispered.

"What?" Laurel glanced at her grandmother, her cheeks burning at the knowing expression on Gladys's face.

"Oh, nothing. Just that my vision is still very keen."

"I'm sure it is."

Curt Jackson appeared at her side. Laurel watched as students started delivering candy and artwork. They didn't need her help. The teens were obviously the best gift the residents had received in a long time. Laurel had no doubt the memories of the teens bringing Christmas to the Manor would live on for a good long time.

"It's good to see you still here," Curt said.

"I'm leaving at the end of the week."

"Before Christmas?" he asked.

She wanted to move past the small talk, to get to the real emotions. The holidays, the weather, her return to Chicago—none of that really mattered. Here was the man who she could have called Dad but he hadn't been a part of her life. She couldn't go from anger to acceptance so quickly.

"I have to get back. I'm starting classes, to finish my degree."

"I see." His gaze slid past her to Gladys.

"Why don't the two of you take a walk?" Gladys suggested.

"Good idea." Laurel kissed her grandmother on the cheek. "I'll be right back."

"I'm obviously not going anywhere." Gladys smiled secretively. "Yet."

"Gran…"

"Oh, go on."

Laurel walked down the hall, next to her father. Father. She didn't know if she ever would call him that. Curt Jackson. If things had been different she would have been Laurel Jackson.

"I know this is difficult," Curt said as he motioned her into a small sitting room. "But I can't tell you how glad I am that we've been able to meet. I want you to know that I am sorry for the way we hurt you, your mother and I. We were young and not thinking about the future. I know my explanations won't change anything, but I do want you to know that I'm sorry."

Laurel pulled two dollars from her purse and fed them to the vending machine. It gave her a minute to think as she selected a bottle of water. "I understand mistakes were made. But I'm not a mistake."

"No, you're definitely *not* a mistake. Your mom raised a strong, intelligent woman. I'm proud of that, of you. I wish I could take some credit for the person standing in front of me."

"If just once you had called, asked to meet me, anything. I get that you were married, and I understand you didn't want to hurt your wife. But I'm the daughter you hurt instead."

His sigh was ragged with emotion. "I know. And if I had been a better person back then, I would have thought about that. I should have shown your mother more respect."

"Thank you for that." Laurel sat down across from him. "I know that things happen for a reason. I'll probably look back on these weeks and know that my life is different because we met. Right now it just hurts."

"I hope that moving forward we find some peace with each other, with God, and with this situation."

"Me, too." She stood. "I need to get back to my grandmother now."

They walked down the hall together, talking about more inconsequential things. But the little details, those were the building blocks of a relationship.

This trip had changed everything for her. Her heart ached a little when she thought of leaving this place, the people. And as they walked into the activity room, she made eye contact with the person she hadn't expected to meet. The man currently at the center of a crowd of teens.

She would definitely miss Cameron Hunt.

Cameron attached a lead rope to the gelding's halter and led him to the small arena. The horse belonged to Gladys. The very same horse that had thrown her. He'd been telling himself for weeks that it wasn't his business but he'd decided to stop lying to himself. Gladys was his business. She was more than his landlady—she was his friend.

Today seemed like a good day to work the animal. After the visit to Lakeside Manor he'd come home restless. There were times that the days were endless. Each day rolled into the next day with nothing to distinguish one from the other. At thirty-five years old, he knew there had to be more to his life.

He thought what he felt might be God pushing him, preparing him for the next chapter in his life.

The horse tugged on the lead rope. He kept a firm hand, walking next to the horse, making the animal slow his pace to Cameron's. The gelding wasn't a bad animal, he just had bad habits. He would get the bit in his teeth and when he did, Gladys couldn't control him. He fought the reins and she sometimes just let him go wherever he wanted. Even on the lead rope, he thought he was the boss.

"We're going to come to an understanding, Buck." He led the horse to the center of the arena and patted his neck. "Buck? Who names a gray horse 'Buck'?"

The horse pushed his big head against Cameron's shoulder. Cameron corrected him and stepped away.

"What are you doing with him?"

The voice took him by surprise. He hadn't heard her approach and was positioned so he couldn't see the fence. He moved, drawing the horse with him.

Laurel stood at the fence, her dark blue coat buttoned tight, her head covered by a gray knit cap. The weather had grown colder throughout the day and a few flurries had fallen, melting as soon as they touched the ground.

"I thought I might try to help him overcome some of his bad habits. I'm hoping she won't ride him but maybe he'll be easier to handle."

"You've got a saddle on him."

"I'm brave," he said, and winked. It was the last thing he expected to do.

"Of course you are."

He put his hand on the horse's neck, soothing the animal as he started to stomp, impatient to move.

"Yes, I thought I might ride him in the arena, just to see how he behaves."

"Be careful."

He grinned at the warning. "No worries, I'm always careful."

Her cheeks flamed and she gave him a sheepish smile. "Silly for someone who has never ridden to tell you, a person who obviously has, to be careful."

"My dad liked to brag that we rode before we walked. I don't know how true that is, but I can't remember a time when I didn't know how to ride."

He studied her for a minute and noticed that her gaze never connected with his. She was avoiding something or was worried.

"What's wrong?" he asked.

"I'm just worried about Rose. She's so settled here. What if they don't allow her to stay?"

He led the horse to the fence that separated them. "We can't change anything by worrying."

"You're right."

He brushed a tendril of hair that had blown across her cheek. She sought his eyes and he knew the questions he saw there. But he didn't have an answer. There was something between them, something sweet and new.

Slowly, she stepped back, putting distance between them.

The moment slipped away, as tenuous as a warm day in midwinter.

"So ride him," she challenged.

"You think I can't?" he laughed, as he led the horse back to the center of the arena. "I'll show you, and him, who's boss."

She quirked an eyebrow at him.

"Don't make a fool of me," he whispered to the horse. Buck twitched an ear.

Cameron tugged on the girth strap, making sure it was tight. He placed the reins over the horse's head and placed his left foot in the stirrup. Buck sidestepped, then took a jarring step forward. Cameron spoke to him and held the reins steady.

"We're not going to play this game."

He waited until Buck stopped moving, then he mounted, swinging his right leg over the animal's broad back. Buck leaped forward and Cameron brought him back with a tug of the reins.

"No, thank you, Buck. I'm not going to the hospital today."

"She needs to get rid of him," Laurel called out as the horse pranced across the arena.

"You think?" He tried to laugh but the horse didn't give

a guy a chance to joke, or even take a breath. He kept his legs tight but let the horse move forward in an easy trot.

He rode him around the arena several times. Then a door banged. The horse nearly shot out from under him but Cameron managed to keep his seat and bring the horse back to a walk. He spoke to the animal in soothing tones, but all the while he cursed the eye he'd lost in Afghanistan. It did him no good to rail against the loss because he knew it wouldn't bring back his sight.

It didn't mean that at least once a day he didn't feel the loss.

"Are you okay?" Laurel called out.

He heard the anxiety in her voice. Her fear. He reined the horse in and headed in her direction. The animal handled surprisingly well, with just the slightest touch of the reins to his neck and the gentlest touch of his knee.

When he could see her, he smiled. "I'm fine. A little adrenaline rush, nothing more. You don't think Rose did that on purpose, do you?"

"Why would she do that?"

He chuckled. "Obvious reasons. She would want me injured and you taking care of me."

"I don't think she would do that." She caught his expression of disbelief. "Would she?"

"Of course she wouldn't. Gladys said she's coming home sooner rather than later. I guess that means you'll be leaving soon?"

She placed her hands on the rail of the corral and rested her chin on her interlaced fingers. Her look was thoughtful as she gazed off in the direction of the lake.

"I have to go. But I'm worried, and I know my grandmother is just as worried, about Rose and the court date."

He swung his right leg over the horse and landed easily on the ground, the horse shifting away from him just a bit. He held the reins tight as he walked up to the fence.

"I know she's worried." He studied the face of the woman standing before him, her hazel eyes bright in the cool winter air. "If you stayed, it might make things easier on her."

"I can't stay. I'm already enrolled in school. I have to pack up my apartment and move back in with my mother. Not exactly something I expected to do at age thirty."

"You talk a lot about what you *have* to do. But I'm not so sure you want to do those things. Why not stay here and apply for a job at the local school? Jack West said there's an opening."

"Yes, Kylie West told me the same thing. But I've never taught before. I got my degree and then went into catering instead."

"It's never too late to go back."

"Sometimes it is, Cameron. Sometimes you have to move forward."

"You're right." He kissed her cheek, pausing there close to her and wanting to say more. "Sometimes you have to know when to let go." He stepped back and nodded in the direction of the house. "Rose is on her way out here. She has lights. I am guessing you'll spend the evening decorating. The house is starting to look like the North Pole exploded in there."

"I'm so glad she's having fun."

"You've been good for her."

"My grandmother is good for her," she argued. It wasn't her best argument. They both knew the truth.

"I'll talk to you later. I have to give this guy a good brushing and some oats." He walked away, leading the big gray, and wishing he could be one of those men who knew the right thing to say at the right time.

And this happened to be one of those times he wanted the courage to say what he really felt.

Chapter Nine

Wednesday evening Laurel stood at the back of the church and watched as Rose practiced her part in the Christmas program. She was dressed like a shepherd, kneeling with the other shepherds, but then she got to her feet and sang a solo about Mary and the baby Jesus.

"She's pretty amazing." Kylie West had entered from the back door and stopped at Laurel's side.

"She is."

Kylie gently cleared her throat. "I don't want to put pressure on you, but did Cameron tell you about the job at the school here?"

"He did. But I can't. I'm registered for classes in Chicago and I…" She hesitated because she didn't know what else to say. That took her by surprise.

Kylie touched her arm. "I understand."

"Thank you." She watched as the practice ended, wishing she could be here for the final performance.

Rose came down off the stage and headed her way wearing her shepherd costume and a big grin. A few other girls joined her.

"Hey, Mom, after we clean up, can we grab a soda at the convenience store?"

Laurel blinked a few times, then it hit her. The other teens were leaving with their parents, talking about plans for the night, for the weekend. And Rose wanted to be one of them.

In a way, she'd been Rose. She'd wanted something she'd never had. A father. That mystery man who had lived in her imagination had finally come to life. He was on the stage, helping to make adjustments to the manger.

"Yes, we can stop at the convenience store," Laurel responded.

Rose gave her a quick hug. "Thank you."

The girl ran off with her friends. Laurel watched her go and returned to her conversation with Kylie.

"Is it healthy for her to do that? Call me 'Mom'?"

Kylie shrugged. "I think so. She wants to fit in but she also wants someone to be the mother she hasn't had. You and Gladys have filled the role."

"I know it seems unfair, or maybe selfish that I'm leaving—I just don't know what else to do. I came here to visit and now it feels as if I should uproot my entire life and relocate here."

"Don't feel guilty, just pray and know that things will work out."

"Thank you." She studied the group of men at the front of the church, laughing with one another and working to make the manger scene perfect.

"I'm going to head out." Kylie gave her a quick hug. "Call me if you need anything."

"Don't worry, I will."

Kylie laughed. "I'm glad."

Laurel watched the other woman leave, then she headed down the aisle of the church. Curt Jackson looked up from the wall he was fastening to the back of the manger. He smiled at her as she approached.

"How did it look from back there?" he asked.

"Really amazing. They all did such a great job."

He set his hammer on the stage. "They're good kids. I grew up in this church."

"I came here with my mother, before we left town."

Silence grew between them and he eventually nodded. "I'm guessing it wasn't easy."

"No, it wasn't. I'm sure there were people who guessed you were my father, but my mother kept her secrets."

"Life is filled with regrets." His tone was quiet and honest. "I have more than my share."

"I'm leaving this weekend." She didn't know what else to say.

"I'm sorry to hear that. But I do hope you'll be back soon and I hope we can continue to talk." He stood up next to her. "I'm looking forward to getting to know you better, Laurel."

"I'd like that." She turned to leave, but his hand on her arm kept her from walking away.

"I'd like to give you a hug, if that's okay." She knew that the ball was in her court. "I have a lot to make up for."

"You do," she agreed. But she took the step that put her close to him and for the first time in her life, she felt her father's embrace. He was strong and maybe it was fanciful, but she felt safe. Protected.

But after a few moments, she pulled away. "I have to go. Rose is waiting for me."

He put two fingers to his brow in a salute. "Until next time, Laurel."

She made it out of the sanctuary before the tears began to fall. She couldn't stop them from trickling down her cheeks. She covered her face with her hands and drew in a deep breath to compose herself.

A hand touched her shoulder, tender and comforting. And then strong arms went around her, pulling her close.

She didn't have to open her eyes to know that it was Cameron. She knew his scent. She knew the strength of his arms. She knew that she'd dreamed of a father, a man who would be her hero. That dream had been replaced by another more dangerous dream, one even less likely to come true. She was dreaming of this man, tall and silent, willing to comfort but unwilling to commit his heart.

"Leaving just got a little more complicated," she told him.

"What happened?" He rubbed her back, kissed the top of her head and then stepped away. "Do I need to hurt someone?"

She gave a soggy laugh. "No, I'm good. Just a conversation with Curt."

"Your father," he added.

"Yes, my father."

"Why are you so determined to leave?" He watched her, his blue eye seeing more than she thought anyone had ever seen. "Are you running?"

"Probably. It's what I've done my whole life. Get close and then back away before I can get hurt. I feel like that started when we left Hope to start a new life in Chicago."

"So stay and face it."

"I can't. I have to pack up an entire apartment, five years' worth of my life, by the end of December."

He put more distance between them. Physical and emotional distance. "You're still running."

"From what?" she asked.

"Me," he said so quietly she almost didn't hear the word. He was tall and imposing, handsome and scarred. And he thought she was running from him. Maybe she was, but probably not for the reasons he thought.

Before she could tell him the truth, he walked away.

* * *

Two days later, Cameron was still questioning his sanity. He'd laid himself bare, exposed his emotions to Laurel Adams.

He tossed two bales of hay down from the hayloft of the barn. Then followed them down via the ladder, not tossing himself. He pulled out his pocketknife and cut the rope that held the bales together. The two horses that had come in from the corral whinnied to get his attention. They were ready for breakfast.

He grabbed a couple of flakes of hay and walked up to the first stall. The mare slipped her nose over the door of the stall, waiting for hay. Her foal moved in close to her side. He shoved the flake of hay into the hay rack on the side of the stall, checked to make sure the automatic waterers were doing their job and moved on to the next horse. The gray gelding of Gladys's.

The horse shoved his nose at Cameron, wanting his hay. He obliged the animal, then gave his neck a pat, just to annoy the horse. True to form, the animal jerked away.

"Your owner is coming home today." Which meant that Laurel would be leaving town tomorrow.

As if on cue, he heard a car come up the drive, then car doors slamming. He walked out the front of the barn and saw his landlady. She waved, smiling big.

"Cam," she called out. "Come give this old lady a hug."

He headed her way, not wanting to be anything like her horse. He could hug her, say something to Rose, because the girl was out of school for the holidays, and be cool to Laurel.

"Welcome home," he said as he got closer.

"It's so good to be back. Laurel said she put a roast in the oven and she's making homemade bread for dinner.

Curt is joining us at six this evening. You should come on down and eat with us. It's Laurel's last night."

"I would, but I have a meeting at Mercy Ranch. Their Christmas event is tomorrow."

"Well, I hate to hear that you can't join us. We'll miss you." Gladys squeezed his arm. "How's my horse. Not starving himself from depression, is he?"

"Hardly," he said. Then he realized what he'd said. "I mean, of course. He's very despondent without you."

She cackled. "We both know that isn't true. That horse is like some men, he cares only about himself."

"Ouch," Cameron said and grabbed his heart.

"Oh, don't worry, you're not one of those men." She glanced from him to her house. "I'm going in now. I sure have missed my house."

"I'm sure you have. Let me know if you need anything."

She waved Laurel and Rose ahead of her. "Give me a minute of your time. Laurel and Rose, you too go on in. Cam will walk me to the door."

Laurel took Rose by the arm, and the two of them headed for the house, their steps slow and reluctant. At the door, Laurel glanced back. Gladys waved her on inside.

"What's up?" Cameron asked.

Gladys sighed. "I'm needing a Christmas gift like no other, Cam."

"What's the matter?"

She pursed her lips, the sign of a woman with a lot on her mind. "Rose's caseworker, Carlie, called me yesterday. She's very worried that they're going to move Rose to a foster home. I never thought riding that horse would change everything for us."

"I'm sorry, Gladys."

She patted his arm. "I know you are. I want you to do something for me."

"Okay, what can I do?"

"Be my lawyer."

"I'm not a lawyer. Not in Oklahoma."

"Then be one. You're as bad as my granddaughter, hiding from who you really are. Yes, you're training some nice horses. Is that enough to fulfill your life?"

"I'm not sure, Gladys. For the past few years, it has been."

"I know you needed time to heal…" She took a few steps away from him and paused, her hand clenching at her side.

"Gladys, are you okay?"

She nodded but kept walking. "I'm fine. I'm just not used to all of this excitement."

He took her at her word but couldn't help but feel there was more to it. He caught up with her, trying to pretend he wasn't there to help her up the back steps of her house. She gave him a narrow-eyed look that said she knew exactly what he was up to.

"Stop acting as if I'm a feeble old lady."

He didn't say anything, just offered his arm.

"Fine," she grumbled. "But just to make you feel good about yourself. And because it wouldn't hurt my granddaughter to take a good look at what she's leaving behind."

He should have walked away while he had the chance. Instead he found himself being led into the house by Gladys's iron grip on his hand.

As they walked into the kitchen, the aroma of roast and potatoes made his mouth water and reminded him he'd skipped breakfast. Laurel was standing at the counter, measuring water into a bowl and pouring in a packet of yeast. Gladys had mentioned that her granddaughter was making bread. Rose was right next to her, asking questions about the process.

"Look who decided to have coffee with us," Gladys said, all chipper. "My favorite neighbor."

Laurel looked up, as if she was surprised to see him with her grandmother. "Oh, Cameron."

"Yes, Cameron." Gladys patted his arm and let go to take a seat at the counter. "Do we have coffee?"

"We do." Laurel gave her grandmother a wary look. He guessed he wasn't the only one who thought Gladys was obvious in her attempts at matchmaking. "Do you want some Christmas cookies to go with that?"

Rose grabbed a container off the counter. "We made them last night. We found your cookie cutters and made all sorts of shapes. And they're iced, too."

The teen took the lid off the container and presented an assortment of stars, bells, and trees.

Cameron sat next to Gladys and he said his own prayer for a Christmas blessing.

He either had to let Laurel go, or make her realize that she was meant to stay in Hope, to be here with Gladys and Rose—and him.

Chapter Ten

❧

Laurel left early the next morning. There were tearful goodbyes with both Rose and her grandmother, but she promised to come back soon. That didn't seem to make them feel any better. And Cameron didn't show up to tell her goodbye. She reminded herself not to be surprised or hurt by that.

She'd done her best to push him away. After all, it was safer to be the one pushing others away than to be the one hurt when someone walked out of her life.

The farther she drove from Hope, the more her heart ached at the idea of being almost seven hundred miles away. She kept telling herself all of the reasons she had to go. First, she could no longer afford her apartment, and that meant moving out in the next week and moving back in with her mother.

Second, she was going back to college.

Tears gathered in her eyes as she thought about everything she'd left behind. She'd never felt a loss so deeply.

It was late in the evening when she pulled up to her mother's house in the Chicago suburbs. The lights were on and she could see the Christmas tree through the open curtains of the living room window. She parked and got out, taking her time gathering her bags.

Her mom met her at the door with a welcoming hug. Patricia Adams stepped back, taking one of the bags as she did. "Come in. I've missed you so much."

"I've missed you, too." She stepped into the living room and set down her bag on the floor.

She couldn't stop the tears that began to flow.

"Honey, what in the world is wrong?"

Laurel shook her head. "I'm just… I didn't expect…"

"To miss them when you left?"

She nodded and grabbed a tissue out of the box on the table. "Yes. How did you do it?"

"I did it for you. And for me. I wanted us to have a fresh start somewhere where no one knew us."

"I met him, you know."

"I know—he called me."

Anger got mixed up with the hurt. "How often do the two of you talk? You know I'm thirty, not three. You could have told me his name. You could have warned me he would be there."

"I know. I'm sorry. I should have." Her mom sat down on the couch and patted the spot next to her. "I should have told you about him."

"Would've been nice."

"He broke my heart. I broke my own heart, too. Then I broke my mother's heart. And I hurt you because you were the one most affected by my choices. But I love you and I've done everything I could to give you a good life."

"And you did. I am glad you gave me life."

"I hope you'll forgive me. Forgive us, Curt and me, for what we did to you."

"I love you and I forgive you. I'm just tired from the drive, I think."

Her mom studied her face for a long time. "Well, I suspect this has something to do with Rose, and a lot to do with my mother's handsome tenant."

"You and Gran both make mountains out of molehills."

"You're even talking like her now," her mother noted.

"Hmm, could be." Laurel was fading fast. "I hope you won't be hurt if I go to bed now. It's been a long day."

"That's fine, but before you go to bed, I need to talk to you."

"This sounds serious," Laurel wiped at her eyes with the tissue. "I'm not sure if I'm ready."

"You're going to have to be. I've put this off for years, but I think it's time for me to move back to Hope. I'm going to work another six months at the hospital here, but I've talked to the hospital in Grove and also to Dr. West in Hope. There are job opportunities and I really want to go home."

Laurel wasn't surprised. After spending time with her grandmother in Hope, it seemed like the best plan.

"I'm sure Gran is over the moon about that."

"She is," her mom agreed. "But how do *you* feel about me leaving? I know you're set to begin classes and you thought you'd be living here with me."

"Will you want to sell the house? Because I can start looking for an apartment."

Her mom gave her a thoughtful look. "Eventually I will have to sell but you can stay here for now. Are you okay with this, Laurel?"

"It's a big change but I'll adjust."

She kissed her mother on the cheek, and headed to her old bedroom. But she got to thinking—if both her mother and grandmother were going to be in Hope, what was left for her in Chicago?

The phone rang early the next morning. Laurel listened as her mom answered. She couldn't hear the conversation but she heard the concern in her mother's voice. A moment later there was a knock on the door.

"Come in."

Her mom stepped into her room, her face pale. "Your grandmother had a heart attack last night. It was mild, but she's in the hospital."

"What about Rose?" Laurel was already out of bed.

"With the Wests. It was Cameron who called. He's going to the hospital this morning and he was there last night. But he said the caseworker is aware of what happened. She'll try to leave Rose with the Wests for Christmas but she can't guarantee she'll be able to make that happen."

Laurel grabbed her suitcase. "We have to go."

"I know. But, Laurel, we can't stop them from taking Rose."

Laurel closed her eyes. "I know. But I have to be there. For Gran, and for Rose. I want to at least be there to let her know that we care and we'll do what we can for her."

"What can we do?" Laurel's mom asked. "We live in Chicago. Your grandmother's heart attack was mild but I don't think they're going to let her continue to foster a teenager, even if she is family."

"Mom, do you think God allows things like this to happen in order to help us find the right path?"

Her mom paused at the doorway. "Sometimes, honey. Maybe we've been on the right path but God is showing us a different direction. Where is your path taking you?"

"I'm not really sure. But I think we should get the earliest flight possible, and take our Christmas gifts with us. I think we'll be having Christmas in Oklahoma this year."

The door to Gladys's hospital room opened. Cameron looked up, not surprised to see Laurel, Rose and an older woman who resembled Gladys. Rose remained close to

Laurel's side. Hopefully Family Services would wait until after Christmas to move Rose to another home. He understood that the county didn't feel it was in Rose's best interests to be left in the care of a woman who seemed to be having significant health problems. He prayed that whatever solution they found, it would be best for the girl.

As long as they didn't make her spend Christmas with strangers.

"Well, look who's here!" Gladys sat up a little. "I hope you're here to break me out of this place. I've had it with hospitals and being confined to the indoors."

"Mother, I doubt anyone wants you out of here more than the nurses." Laurel's mother hugged Gladys. "You look good, Mom."

"I *am* good. They did the stents. I'm fine and ready to go home."

"I'm sure you are. Tomorrow."

Gladys sighed and leaned back on her pillow. "Rose, come hug me. You're the only reasonable one in the bunch."

Rose hurried forward and hugged her. Then Laurel stepped forward.

Gladys held out a hand to her granddaughter. "Oh, stop looking so wounded. I promise you I didn't do this just to bring you back."

Laurel smiled. "I did kind of wonder if you had the ability to make yourself sick just to get me back to Hope."

Gladys laughed, then shifted her attention back to Rose. "Don't look so down, little chick, we'll figure this out."

"I don't want to leave," Rose sobbed and buried her face in Gladys's shoulder. "You're all I've got."

Cameron stood, offering his seat to Laurel's mother. He needed some air because this child who desperately needed a family was going to break his heart. He wanted to fix everything for her. But how could he? He was a single man.

They weren't going to allow him to take her in. His gaze touched on Laurel. He thought she might be the only person who could fix this for Rose.

He wanted her to be the person he thought she was, but he worried that she didn't know that about herself. She didn't see the person he saw.

He settled his gaze on her, on the generous mouth, the sprinkling of freckles on her nose, the hair that reminded him of autumn. If he missed her this much after one day, he didn't see a lot of hope for next week or the week after.

"Ladies, I'm going to head out," he told the three women as he headed for the door.

"Don't you dare sell my horse while I'm in here," Gladys warned.

"I wouldn't dream of it. I've gotten kind of attached to him."

Gladys gave him a fond smile, then her gaze shifted to her granddaughter. Laurel looked at him, her expression unreadable. But she followed him out the door.

"Thank you, Cameron," she said once they were in the hall.

"She's more than my landlady or neighbor, Laurel, she's my friend."

"I know. I'm glad she has you. If she'd been alone…"

"She wasn't." He resisted the urge to brush strands of red hair away from her face. "I'll take care of her livestock for the next few days."

"We appreciate that. We'll be here a few days. You should come to dinner on Christmas."

"I might. Jack invited me out to Mercy Ranch. Maria is a good cook, but…"

Her mouth tilted in a half grin. "What you're saying is— it's about who might serve the better meal?"

"A man does need to think about those things." He touched his fingers to hers. "I have to go."

He walked away, thanking God above he hadn't made a fool of himself. He wasn't the kind of man that begged a woman to stay, but she was definitely the kind of woman who would make him reconsider.

Chapter Eleven

Laurel drove to church with her grandmother sitting next to her in the front seat, and Rose and Laurel's mother in the back seat. It was Christmas Eve. Gladys had been released from the hospital the previous day. For the first time in years, the three of them were together for Christmas. Four if you counted Rose. Laurel only hoped something would happen that would keep Rose in their lives.

As they pulled into the church parking lot, she spotted Carlie's car. The caseworker waved as they pulled in next to her. What brought a caseworker out on Christmas Eve? Hopefully she wasn't there to remove Rose from their home.

Her grandmother murmured something quietly, asking Jesus to give them peace. From the back seat, Rose sobbed a little.

"She isn't going to take me today, is she?" Rose asked. "She can't take me today. Not before Christmas. She said she wouldn't unless she had to."

"Rose, be calm and trust that God has a plan." Gladys glanced back at the girl. "I know this is frightening but we have to be calm. It won't do us any good if we panic."

"I know." Rose sighed. "I know. But I'm scared."

"I know you are, but no matter what, I'm always going to be your aunt Gladys. We didn't know about one another for a lot of years, but now we do. You're stuck with us, kiddo. We're family."

Laurel parked and they exited the vehicle. Rose hurried to tuck herself in close to Gladys. Carlie smiled at the four of them but her gaze lingered on Rose.

"How are you?" Carlie asked the girl.

"Scared. I don't want to leave. Gladys is still healthier than most people half her age. She can take care of me just fine."

"I know she can, but is it the best thing for both of you, Rose? We're thinking of you but also of Gladys. Raising a teenager is a lot of work." Carlie gave the girl a sympathetic look.

"But I can help her. And I'll be the best-behaved teenager ever." Rose gave Laurel a look that implored her to step in, to plead her case.

Snow started to fall. Big white flakes, the kind that were typically pretty but didn't amount to much in Oklahoma. The world seemed quieter as the snow fell. Laurel could hear the piano begin to play in the sanctuary and the church bells rang, the sound pealing through the stillness of the morning.

Laurel closed her eyes to say a silent prayer for wisdom and guidance. God had laid a new path before her and it was frightening. When she opened her eyes, the other women were looking at her. She smiled.

"I'm staying," she said. "I'm staying in Hope. I'll take guardianship of Rose."

Rose threw her arms around Laurel. Laurel looked at her grandmother and saw tears trickling down her cheeks.

"Is that okay? I've discussed it with God but maybe I should have ran it past you first?"

Gladys laughed. "Oh, honey, we've both been discussing this with God. I think more than one person has prayed you would stay. We've all just been waiting for you to see what was right in front of you."

"Or right there in front of the church waiting for her," Rose giggled as she gave Gladys a big hug.

Laurel glanced at the church entrance and saw him. He was standing by the double doors, the snow falling around him. She didn't see the scars, the patch, or even the perfect side of his face—she saw him. She saw a man that she had fallen in love with.

"Will it work, if I'm the guardian?" Laurel asked Carlie.

The social worker looked from Rose to Gladys to Laurel. "I'm hopeful. I obviously don't have the authority to make that decision on my own, but I don't see why it couldn't work."

The bells rang, the sound echoing in the snowy morning.

"We should all go in," Laurel's mom said, taking her mother by the arm to help her walk along on the snow-covered sidewalk. "Join us, Carlie?"

"I would like to. I haven't lived here for very long and I've missed going to church." Carlie moved to Gladys's other side.

"Then you should definitely come on in and be a part of our church family." Gladys reached out with her free hand. Carlie stepped closer to Laurel's grandmother's side and the three of them were on their way.

Laurel followed, still coming to terms with what she'd just decided. Her whole life would change. She knew that. But it felt right.

This felt like God's plan for her. And the timing was perfect. It was Christmas, a time for new beginnings.

Cameron watched as the women in the parking lot headed his way. Rose ran ahead of them. Gladys walked up the sidewalk escorted by her daughter and the caseworker. Laurel followed a short distance behind them.

Rose hurried across the parking lot, sliding a little on the slippery snowflakes.

"Be careful," he called out to her.

"I am. I just want to get inside and tell everyone the news. I got my Christmas prayer answered."

"A Christmas prayer is it?" he asked as he reached for her hand and led her up the steps.

"Yeah, and you can thank me later." She laughed as she ran past him into the church. Cheeky kid.

Gladys came next. She stopped to hug him and tell him that God had a way of working things out for the best. He helped her into the church, then returned to the steps to wait for Laurel.

The snow kept falling, the flakes getting bigger. Big flakes clung to Laurel's hair, her coat. She smiled up at him.

Inside the church, the piano music started. "Silent Night." He walked down the steps toward the woman who had stolen his heart. She was his music. Would it be too much to tell her that? She calmed him. She made him feel like he could get through the nightmares.

"I didn't think it would snow like this in Oklahoma," she said. "But Rose said she'd been praying for a white Christmas."

"It seems Rose prays for a lot of things."

She laughed. "And if God doesn't answer, Rose takes it upon herself to help Him."

"I warned you she was Capital T."

"Yes, you did." She reached out and touched his cheek. "I missed you."

"You were only gone for a day." The words came out rougher than he had intended.

"Feels like I've been gone forever." She looked up at him, her eyes damp with unshed tears. "Is there a chance?"

"A chance?" he asked.

"A chance that there is really an us. I'm tired of reinventing myself, Cameron. I know who I am. I'm a girl from Hope, Oklahoma. And I'm the woman who loves you."

"Laurel Adams, I've been waiting my whole life to meet you."

She laughed and cried a little, then he picked her up and swung her around in his arms. The snow continued to fall, making the world soft and silent, the way only a heavy snowfall could do. He lowered her to the ground and kissed her.

"I love you, Laurel Adams. I'm so glad you came back. Rose and I were praying you would understand how much we want you to be a part of our lives."

"I'm staying. Rose needs me."

"I need you, too."

"Back at ya, cowboy. I couldn't imagine life in Chicago knowing that you're here. And I'd like very much if you'd kiss me again."

"I will." He pulled her into his arms, kissing her until someone shouted to them that they were missing church. They both laughed as he kissed her again. Then, hand in hand, they walked up the church steps and into the cozy, dimly lit sanctuary.

Together.

* * * * *

Dear Reader,

Thank you for joining me in Hope, Oklahoma, for the Christmas season! Although it is a fictional town, I believe Hope is a symbol of all that is right in our world. A community where people come together, helping their neighbors and showing love to those in need.

This holiday season, take a little bit of Hope with you! Reach out to those around you and be a light that shines! Wishing you all the best and a Merry Christmas!

With Love!

Brenda Minton

"FAST FIVE" READER SURVEY

Your participation entitles you to:
✳ Up to 4 FREE BOOKS and Thank-You Gifts Worth Over $20!

Complete the survey in minutes.

Romance

Suspense

Get Up to 4 **FREE Books**

Your Thank-You Gifts include up to **4 FREE BOOKS** and **2 Mystery Gifts**. There's no obligation to purchase anything!

See inside for details.

Dear Reader,

Since you are a lover of our books, your opinions are important to us... and so is your time.

That's why we made sure your **"FAST FIVE" READER SURVEY** can be completed in just a few minutes. Your answers to the five questions will help us remain at the forefront of women's fiction.

And, as a thank-you for participating, we'd like to send you up to **4 FREE BOOKS** and **FREE THANK-YOU GIFTS!**

Try **Love Inspired® Romance Larger-Print** books featuring Christian characters facing modern-day challenges.

Try **Love Inspired® Suspense Larger-Print** novels featuring Christian characters facing challenges to their faith... and lives.

Or **TRY BOTH!**

Enjoy your gifts with our appreciation,

Pam Powers

To get up to
4 FREE BOOKS & THANK-YOU GIFTS:

✳ Quickly complete the "Fast Five" Reader Survey
and return the insert.

"FAST FIVE" READER SURVEY

1 Do you sometimes read a book a second or third time? ○ Yes ○ No

2 Do you often choose reading over other forms of entertainment such as television? ○ Yes ○ No

3 When you were a child, did someone regularly read aloud to you? ○ Yes ○ No

4 Do you sometimes take a book with you when you travel outside the home? ○ Yes ○ No

5 In addition to books, do you regularly read newspapers and magazines? ○ Yes ○ No

YES! Please send me my Free Rewards, consisting of **2 Free Books from each series I select** and **Free Mystery Gifts**. I understand that I am under no obligation to buy anything, as explained on the back of this card.

❏ **Love Inspired® Romance Larger-Print** (122/322 IDL GNSN)
❏ **Love Inspired® Suspense Larger-Print** (107/307 IDL GNSN)
❏ **Try Both** (122/322 & 107/307 IDL GNSY)

FIRST NAME   LAST NAME

ADDRESS

APT.#   CITY

STATE/PROV.   ZIP/POSTAL CODE

READER SERVICE—Here's how it works:

▲ If offer card is missing write to: Reader Service, P.O. Box 1341, Buffalo, NY 14240-8531 or visit www.ReaderService.com ▲

BUSINESS REPLY MAIL
FIRST-CLASS MAIL   PERMIT NO. 717   BUFFALO, NY

POSTAGE WILL BE PAID BY ADDRESSEE

READER SERVICE
PO BOX 1341
BUFFALO NY 14240-8571

NO POSTAGE
NECESSARY
IF MAILED
IN THE
UNITED STATES

A MERRY
WYOMING CHRISTMAS

Jill Kemerer

To Wendy Paine Miller,
my friend for the long haul. I'm so thankful
to have you in my life. Merry Christmas!

Trust in the Lord with all thine heart;
and lean not unto thine own understanding.
—*Proverbs* 3:5

Chapter One

What a way for Sunrise Bend to welcome him back.

Michael Carr leaned forward to concentrate on the highway. It wouldn't be December in Wyoming without icy roads and whiteout conditions. Heavy snow against the night sky kept visibility to a minimum as a gust of wind hit his truck. He adjusted the steering wheel and eased his foot off the accelerator.

Keep it steady. You're almost home.

Home.

He hadn't had one of those in six years.

A sense of yearning hollowed out his chest. His transient life must be catching up to him. Or Christmas being a week away was messing with his head.

He missed the family ranch. Until recently, he hadn't fully appreciated his roots. He craved quiet mornings feeding cattle with his dad and afternoons checking pregnant cows and moving the herd. He pined for the cowboy life he'd left behind after high school, even though he'd been gaining a good reputation for his research as a wildlife biologist.

Moving from location to location was getting old.

If things were different, Michael would be tempted to

move back and partner with his dad on the ranch. But things weren't different, and Michael couldn't pretend his brother's betrayal didn't still hurt. He and David had barely spoken to each other in years, and this Christmas wouldn't change it. Michael just hoped he wouldn't have to spend a second more than necessary with David, Kelli or their three small kids.

Kelli. Thinking of her hardly hurt anymore.

His ex-girlfriend was living proof he'd been a fool to think he could hold a woman's interest with his quiet personality and loner lifestyle.

His windshield wipers were barely keeping up with the snow. Michael could just make out the Welcome to Sunrise Bend sign up ahead. But something was below it, something that didn't belong—a car covered in several inches of snow.

It must have slid off the road earlier and crashed sideways into the signposts. He hoped nobody was inside. With the temperatures dropping to single digits, hypothermia was a real danger. Most people in these parts knew to prep their vehicles with blankets, water and food. Given the angle of the car, Michael couldn't rule out an injury.

He slowed the truck to a crawl and pulled onto the shoulder. Then he grabbed a flashlight from the console, zipped his coat and put on his heavy-duty gloves. After checking for oncoming traffic—thankfully, no one else seemed to be on the road—he climbed out of his truck, braced himself against the wind and trudged through a foot of snow to the car. Pointing the flashlight into the windows, he tried to detect anyone inside.

A woman was in there, and she had a small child bundled on her lap.

He hoped neither of them was hurt.

Lord, let me have found them in time.

* * *

Please, Lord Jesus, send someone to help us…

Shivering uncontrollably, Leann Bowden tucked her chin to rest on the top of her two-year-old daughter's head. It had been hours since Leann's compact car had skidded out of control before crashing into the sign. Not the best start to her new life in Wyoming.

But it could have been worse. She and Sunni could have been injured. Not counting the shooting pains in her wrist and the dull ache in her shoulder, Leann was fine. And Sunni showed no signs of being hurt. The car, on the other hand, would need serious repairs. And she didn't care. A vehicle could be replaced. Her precious daughter could not.

Earlier, she'd gotten out to inspect the damage. The car was wedged tightly against the sign. Two flat tires had sealed her fate. She'd kept the engine idling for heat, but the gas had run out long ago and her cell phone had no service. As the temperatures had dropped, she'd moved to the passenger side for more room, pulled Sunni onto her lap and wrapped her in every blanket and sweater she could find. Thankfully, Sunni was a sweet-natured child and hadn't made a fuss.

The cold seeped clear through to Leann's bones, and she wrapped her arms more tightly around her sleeping little girl. Every muscle in her body ached with tension. It had been a long day, a long ride. Exhaustion kept pulling down her eyelids. Sheer fear kept her from letting herself give in to sleep.

If someone didn't find her and Sunni soon, they would freeze.

A knocking sound came from the window. Her heart jumped to her throat. Someone was out there. Someone had found them!

Thank You, Lord!

"Can you unlock the door?" The words were low, muffled.

Leann scrambled to press the unlock button, and the door opened. Wind and snow blew inside, snapping the final thread on her self-control. A flashlight beamed her way, and she shielded her eyes against the bright light.

"Are you okay?" The man's voice sounded rough, like he hadn't spoken in a while.

"I've been praying for you to come," she said softly.

He turned off the flashlight and pocketed it. "Are you injured?"

"No."

"Hand me the baby." He held his arms out.

With the flashlight no longer blinding her, she briefly studied him. A stocking cap covered his hair, and he wore a work jacket she'd expect to see on a cowboy. From the looks of it, this guy was about the same age as her. Maybe a few years older. The outdoorsy type.

Nothing like her ex-husband, that was for sure.

Leann winced as she attempted to pass Sunni out to him, but he easily picked up her daughter then held out his hand to her.

"I think I can do it." She grabbed her purse and the tote with Sunni's supplies. "Oh! I forgot about the car seat."

"Let's get you two into my truck where it's warm. I'll come back for the car seat." He carefully took her by the arm and helped her navigate to his truck. The blowing snow stung her cheeks. Then he opened the door, boosted her up and handed Sunni to her. "Did you hit your head? Does anything feel broken?"

"No." From inside the truck, she got a better look at him. Deep blue eyes. Broad shoulders. And handsome. Very handsome. His expression was closed off, but she could sense his concern.

"I'll be right back." He gave her a firm nod. "Do you need anything else out of the car?"

Did she? Her suitcase would be nice, but it was probably asking for too much. She looked around and didn't see Sunni's favorite stuffed animal.

"Bumbles." Leann's teeth chattered. Her body would not stop shivering.

"What?" He leaned closer. "How long were you out there? You might have hypothermia."

"It's my daughter's stuffed rabbit. She must have dropped it when she fell asleep." She handed him her keys.

His face cleared. "Okay. Nothing else?"

"There's a suitcase in the trunk. If you could get it, it would be a big help, but don't worry about—"

"I'll get it." He shut her door and disappeared.

The warmth of the truck sent stabbing sensations to her frozen fingers and toes. Sunni had slept through the commotion. Leann kissed the top of her head again.

Today hadn't gone as planned, but it didn't matter. In a few weeks, this would be a distant memory, and Leann would be managing The Sassy Lasso, a women's Western boutique her friend from college Kelli Carr owned. In the meantime, Leann and Sunni would stay at the local bed-and-breakfast until they found an apartment. She couldn't wait to explore the town and get in the Christmas spirit.

Goodbye, St. Louis. Hello, Sunrise Bend.

Christmas was going to be wonderful this year.

After the previous couple of holiday seasons, Leann was due for a good one. Right after Sunni was born two years ago, her husband, Luke, left her for Deb, a beautiful dentist at his practice. And last summer, Luke and Deb had wed and promptly relocated to Costa Rica. Luke had claimed he wanted to be part of Sunni's life, but how could he be involved with their daughter if he lived in another country? The man was all talk, no action. At least he paid generous child support.

Her door opened, and the man handed her Bumbles along with her keys. He shut her door, then stowed the suitcase in the back seat.

"How does the car seat go in?" he asked.

"I'll do it. It's kind of tricky."

"You're freezing. Just tell me what to do."

"Pull the strap…" She explained how to lock the seat into place. "I'll get her buckled in."

As she reached for the door handle, she winced again.

"Let me." He opened her door and gently lifted Sunni off her lap. Leann told him where the straps went and how to check to make sure everything was tight enough. In no time flat, he'd gotten Sunni settled. Then he hopped back into the driver's seat, shifted into Drive and carefully pulled back onto the road.

"Is she okay?" He glanced back at Sunni.

"I think so. She's been sleeping. By the way, I'm Leann, and that's my two-year-old daughter, Sunni. Thank you for stopping. I was so worried. We never would have made it through the night if you hadn't helped us. I can't thank you enough."

"It's no trouble. I'm Michael." He drove slowly, paying close attention to the road. "Where are you headed?"

"Sunrise Bend. I have a reservation at the bed-and-breakfast in town."

"Dandy's, I assume? It's not far."

"Yes, Dandy's." She tried to ignore the prickling pain creeping through her body as the heat blasted her. She couldn't wait to change into her warmest pajamas and crawl under the covers.

"What about you?" she asked. "Where are you going?"

"Same as you. Sunrise Bend. My family owns a ranch outside town."

"Oh, do you live there?"

"No, just visiting for the holidays."

Why disappointment settled in her gut, she couldn't say. *Oh, really, Leann? You don't know why you're disappointed this attractive guy is only in town for the holidays?*

Maybe the storm had frozen her brain. After the divorce, she'd promised herself she wouldn't so much as look at a guy who didn't plan on sticking around. She and Sunni had already had one man desert them. At this point, her only goal was to set down some roots and give Sunni a happy life. Dating could wait…indefinitely.

"Where do you live?" Her attention was drawn to his profile. Sharp chin. Strong jaw. Straight nose. And those blue eyes.

"Nowhere at the moment. I haven't decided where to work next. I'm a wildlife biologist." He slowed taking the curve, and soon a traffic light came into view. "Almost there."

Leann turned her attention out the window. If it wasn't for Michael, she might not have made it to Sunrise Bend at all. And though he might only be visiting for the holidays, she planned on settling in for the long haul.

She couldn't wait to catch a glimpse of her new home sweet home.

Michael parked as best as he could in front of Dandy's Bed and Breakfast while snow continued to fall. He got out, ducked his chin, then rounded the front of the truck.

I've been praying for you to come. The words she'd first said to him kept repeating in his head. Stupid to get so sentimental over one line. Especially since she'd only meant she'd been praying for someone to come. Not necessarily him.

No one really needed *him*.

Her eyes were the palest blue he'd ever seen. And they were trusting. Full of hope and gratitude.

He wasn't used to pretty blue eyes bursting with appreciation for him. And he didn't like the effect they were having on his pulse. The last time he'd fallen for sparkling eyes had been Kelli, and look how that had turned out.

"I'll carry your daughter inside." He helped Leann onto the sidewalk. Then he turned to unbuckle the little girl, Sunni. Cute name. She'd woken up, and her eyes were big and blue like her mama's. She stared at him, studying his face.

"Uh, let's get you out of the seat." To his surprise, she held her arms up. He lifted her easily.

"Bubba!" she cried, pointing to the seat. He turned back. The rabbit. He handed it to her, and, with the little girl tucked against his chest, escorted Leann to the front door.

A bell jingled above them. Light from a chandelier flooded the foyer, and strands of white lights wound up the staircase directly ahead. An antique desk stood to their left, and a Christmas tree beckoned from the living room ahead.

"Terrible night!" Margo Dandy bustled to them from a swinging door which led, he assumed, to the kitchen. She stopped and grinned when she saw him. "Well, if it isn't Mikey C. Come here and give old Margo a hug."

She held her arms out wide. Margo looked the same as she had when he was growing up, except her permed, short hair was white now instead of bleached blond. A bit on the plump side, Margo wore jeans and a gray sweatshirt with cardinals on the front.

After he hugged her, she stepped back. "And who is this? Did you find yourself a girl?"

"I'm Leann Bowden." Her smile was wide, her voice soft. "I have a reservation. Michael was kind enough to stop and help Sunni and me. Our car skidded off the road."

Only then did he notice how pale Leann was and the shivers she was trying to hide. He frowned. She needed to get warm. Immediately.

"Margo, can you get them settled into a room quickly? She was trapped in her car for a long time."

"In this storm? You must be half frozen." Margo grabbed a key off the row of hooks behind the desk and bustled to the staircase with Leann on her heels. "Follow me. I have extra quilts in the closet, and I'll get a pot of tea ready for you in a jiffy…"

"I'll go out and get your suitcase." He started to set Sunni down, but she held on to him tighter. She wasn't shy with him, he'd give her that. Her chubby, rosy cheeks and long, dark lashes made her look more like a doll than a living child.

She was the cutest thing he'd ever seen.

"Bubba." She held up the stuffed rabbit. He patted its head. She hugged it and laid her cheek against his shoulder. His heart puddled into jelly.

Seconds later, Leann hurried back down the steps to him. "I'm so sorry. I didn't mean to leave her."

"Mama." Sunni beamed.

"Come here, sweet one." She tried to take Sunni from him, but at the contact, she gasped and grew even paler.

"You're hurt." He kept his hold on Sunni. "I'll carry her up."

"Thanks." Her smile was full of gratitude. She turned and climbed the stairs, and he followed her and set Sunni on the bed. "I'll get your things."

The snow was still coming down hard as he hauled the suitcase out of the truck. Now what? Leann was clearly injured, but the clinic wouldn't be open tonight. Her car was smashed up. And she had a toddler. He couldn't just leave her to deal with everything on her own.

When he got back indoors, he shook off the snow, borrowed a pen and piece of paper from the pad sitting on the entrance desk and scribbled his cell phone number on it. Then he took the steps two at a time on his way to Leann's room. The door was open, so he set the suitcase down with a light thud. He shifted from one foot to the other in the doorway.

"Oh, thank you, Michael!"

"Fank you, Myco!" Sunni ran to him and hugged his legs. Her wide grin revealed tiny white teeth.

He laughed, ruffling her hair. "You be good for your mama, okay?"

"'Kay." She toddled back to Leann.

"I'll be back tomorrow morning. Here's my number if you need anything." He handed Leann the paper with his cell number. "I'll take care of the car for you. You'll need a doctor to check you out. I can drive you to the clinic if it's open."

Leann's cheeks grew pink. "That's nice of you, but—"

"I'm coming over tomorrow," he said firmly. "Just try to get some rest." Then he winked at Sunni and let himself out.

He wasn't about to let an injured single mother, with no vehicle and no family in town, handle her problems by herself.

Unfortunately, it would mean running into his brother sooner than he'd anticipated.

Michael tromped out to his truck. The whole ranching-with-Dad thing had been a nice fantasy, but there was no way he was moving back to Sunrise Bend. Not with David and Kelli living here, constantly reminding him of what he'd lost. And Leann up there? Like she'd ever consider a boring guy like him. He'd help with her car, take her to the clinic and that was it. Spending additional time with the pretty mom would be flirting with disaster.

Chapter Two

The world glittered with fresh snow. It was pretty. Peaceful.

Leann sipped tea at one of the dining tables the next morning. Sunni was making Bumbles hop along the windowsill of the picture window close to Leann's chair. A snowplow had poked through Main Street once. Not many other vehicles were out and about. Last night Michael had mentioned coming over to help her out, but maybe he was just being nice.

Would he show up this morning?

"Bubba want cookie." Sunni hugged the rabbit tightly.

"He does, huh? Did he eat his eggs like a good bunny?" She eyed the plate of scrambled eggs Sunni had barely touched.

With wide eyes, Sunni nodded.

Leann wasn't falling for her innocent act. "If Bumbles eats three more bites of eggs—big bites—then I think he can have a cookie."

"Bubba not hungwy for eggs. He want cookie."

"No cookie before eggs."

Sunni's bottom lip jutted out, and rather than eating her breakfast, she resumed playing with Bumbles.

After severe chills last night, Leann had fallen into a

deep sleep with Sunni tucked into her side. She'd woken stiff and sore. She couldn't put any weight on her left wrist. Thankfully, Sunni hadn't minded holding her good hand to climb down the stairs this morning. But Leann wasn't sure what she'd do when her daughter's energy ran out. The child would want to be carried, a difficult task given Leann's wrist.

She wouldn't worry about it now. In fact, she wasn't worrying about anything. None of her troubles mattered because she was here. Ready to start the next chapter—a good chapter—in her life. As soon as she found an apartment, she'd call the movers to bring the rest of her stuff and get settled for good, but in the meantime, she'd stay at the B and B. Leann and Sunni seemed to be the only guests at the moment.

Earlier, she'd peeked down the street, and a thrill had rushed through her at the sight of all of the snow-covered awnings above shop doors, strings of Christmas lights stretched across the road and big red bows wrapped around lampposts.

This was her new home, and it was delightful.

The owners of the B and B, Margo and her husband, Felix, had left a note stating breakfast was set up on the dining room buffet, and if she needed anything to help herself. They would be back this afternoon. Apparently, they were checking on Margo's mother, who lived across town.

"Cookie now, Mama?"

Leann pointed to Sunni's abandoned plate full of food. Sunni let out a loud, pitiful sigh, climbed back into her chair and tucked into the eggs. Meanwhile, Leann made a mental list of everything she needed to do in the upcoming days.

First things first. She'd call Kelli to let her know she'd arrived. In the next day or two, she planned on stopping in at The Sassy Lasso to get an overall feel for the store. Then she'd find an apartment and set up childcare for Sunni. When she'd called last week, two day-care centers in town had spots for her daughter.

She frowned. None of this would be easy without her car. Nor did it help that her left arm was basically useless at this point.

"All done." Sunni pointed to her plate. She'd pushed the eggs to the side. Leann checked under the table. Sure enough, there were eggs down there, too.

"I don't think so, sweetheart. Two more bites. Then you need to pick up the food you dropped. We don't want Mrs. Dandy to have to clean up after us."

Pouting, she dutifully ate two more bites, slid down from the chair and got onto her hands and knees to pick up the eggs.

The front door opened, and Michael entered. Leann's heart started thumping. He'd kept his word!

"Myco!" Sunni scampered to her feet and raced to him. To his credit, he grinned and scooped her up.

"Hey, Sunni, how'd you sleep?"

"Good. Bubba get cookie now."

"He does? I want a cookie, too." He carried her to the table and nodded to Leann. "I checked on your car this morning."

"Already?" Leann couldn't get over it. He must have gotten up at the crack of dawn.

Sunni wriggled in his arms to get set down. "Cookie!"

He lowered her, and she ran to the buffet.

"You didn't have to check on my car." But she sure was glad he did. "You're on vacation. You should have slept in."

"Eh, sleep is overrated." His smile lit his eyes.

"Not to me," she teased.

"There's a good auto shop here in town. If you don't

mind giving me your keys, I'll run them over to the shop so they can get your car towed over there as soon as the roads are clear."

One big problem solved. And by a stranger. He'd been so kind to her. "Thank you! It's so generous of you. I'm… well… I don't know what to say."

"It's nothing." His face grew red.

"Why don't you sit down, and I'll get you a cup of coffee?" She gestured to the chair opposite hers.

"Oh… I…I'd better go." He glanced back at the front door. Was he uncomfortable being alone with her?

"Myco!" Sunni bounded over to him with a cookie in each hand. She held one up to him. "Cookie!"

His expression softened. "I guess I could stay for a few minutes." He took the frosted reindeer from Sunni and sat on a chair. She set hers on the table and started climbing onto his lap.

"No, Sunni—" Leann scolded.

"She's fine." His blue eyes met hers, and she caught her breath at the affection within them. He clearly had a soft spot for her little girl. Sunni rested the back of her head against his chest and happily munched on her cookie.

"Thank you." Leann had said it several times since meeting him, and she'd say it a thousand more for the generosity he'd shown her.

"My pleasure."

She couldn't look away from him, and the moment grew long. Too long. Embarrassed, she rose and padded to the coffee maker. "How do you take your coffee?"

"With a little cream."

Forgetting the pain in her wrist, Leann tried to multitask by grabbing a mug with one hand and the coffeepot with the other. Pain shot up her arm. She had to brace herself against the buffet with her good hand. She needed to have a doctor look at her wrist soon. When the throbbing subsided, she carried the mug of coffee over to him.

"So, you grew up around here?" She returned to her seat.

"Yeah. My parents and sister, Hannah, live on our family ranch."

"I'm sure they're thrilled to have you home for Christmas."

"They are. Hannah, especially. She graduated from college this spring and is sending out résumés to the local schools. I haven't seen her in a few months."

"I'm sure it's hard with your job." What was it he said he did again? Wildlife something or other.

"It is. I've been up in Alberta, Canada, all year working on a research project, and I wasn't able to stop in at the university to visit Hannah as often as usual."

"Canada, huh? Do you think you'll go back?"

"No," he said. "My research partner wants me to join her team in Alaska."

His research partner wanted him to join *her* team? A sinking feeling slid down Leann's torso. Her ex-husband had worked closely with brilliant, beautiful Deb, and look how that had worked out. Leann had ended up divorced and alone.

"You don't sound convinced you're going." She kind of hoped he wasn't convinced. Alaska was a long way away, and he was the only person besides Kelli she knew here. But he probably wanted to get back to his research...and his research partner.

"Yeah, well, I haven't decided yet."

"What are your other options?" she asked.

"A buddy of mine who works for the state of Wyoming badgers me every year to become a game warden.

And there are grants I could apply for to research wildlife anywhere in the world. Then there's…ah… Never mind."

"It sounds exciting." What else had he been about to say?

"Exciting?" He chuckled. "I live in rustic cabins in the middle of nowhere." His face brightened as he spoke. "I study fish and track animals in all kinds of weather, and then there are the reports I have to type up…"

"Say what you want—I can tell you love it."

"I've enjoyed it." He took a drink of his coffee. "What about you? What brings you to Sunrise Bend?"

"A new job. I'll be starting right after the New Year. It will give me a few weeks to find an apartment and line up babysitting. I can't wait to explore the area."

"Just you and Sunni?" His eyebrows drew together.

"Yes, it's just us. My ex-husband moved to Costa Rica with his new wife."

"Oh." He rubbed the back of his neck. "I'm sorry."

"It's okay." She shrugged. "I was thrilled when I found out Kelli—she's a friend from college—wanted to spend more time at home with her kids. She hired me to manage The Sassy Lasso. It's a Western women's boutique here in town. But you probably already know of it."

His face went blank. Sunni had finished her cookie and climbed off his lap. The little imp ran back to the buffet.

"No, Sunni, no more cookies. Excuse me a minute." Leann jogged to her daughter and reached down to pick her up. "Ouch!" Once again, she'd forgotten her wrist.

"Mama?" Sunni's eyes filled with tears.

"I'm fine, baby." *Take deep breaths*.

"You need to see a doctor." Michael came up beside her. "Let me make a call." He walked out of the room swiping his phone. She couldn't take her eyes off the tall cowboy.

He was different from her ex. Comfortable in his own

skin. A man of his word. He wasn't trying to impress her, but impress her, he did.

Really, she had to stop with the romantic crush feelings. She had enough to worry about at the moment, like getting her life lined up. And then how she was going to handle working full-time after only working part-time for so long. She'd never had a prestigious career, an outgoing personality or the allure that some women were born with. But she knew how to manage a retail store. She'd managed a clothing store before having Sunni and had been the assistant manager of one since the divorce.

He strolled back into the room. "I'll come back at two. They can get you in then."

For the umpteenth time she said, "Thank you."

Michael had taken a huge burden off her back. She couldn't thank him enough.

Leann was friends with Kelli *and* going to work for her? Michael's brain had been tripping over those two facts ever since he'd left the B and B earlier.

He followed his father out of the stables. They'd finished checking the cattle and were heading back into the main house. He dreaded taking Leann to the clinic. Not because he didn't like her—he hadn't been able to get her off his mind all day—but the doctor at the clinic was his brother. David. Interactions between them tended to be awkward. And Leann would notice and ask questions.

Well, actually, if he were smart, he wouldn't have to see David at all. He'd drop Leann off at the front desk and wait outside for her until she was finished.

If she was friends with Kelli, she probably already knew about the drama that went down years ago. Not a reassuring thought.

"It's good to have you back for a few weeks, son." His

dad, lean and wiry, strode next to him on the snowy path to the house. "This year kicked me in the behind."

"What do you mean?"

"I'm sixty-five and feeling every second of it."

"You're not sick or anything are you?" He cast a sideways glance at his dad, but other than a few more wrinkles on his face and the thinning gray hair under his hat, the man looked as fit as ever.

"No, no. Nothing like that." Dad chuckled. "Your mother and I have been talking about our next phase, though. I don't know how much longer I'll be able to run the ranch on my own."

The words kicked up longings, fear and regrets. "What are you saying? Are you looking to hire a manager or something?"

"Don't know yet." Dad shrugged. "But I can't do this forever."

"You wouldn't sell it, would you?" Michael tried to envision a future without Carr Ranch in it. His heart sank to his toes. The ranch had been an anchor for him all his life. "This is home." His home, at least. He had no other.

"Sell it? Not while I'm still alive." He laughed, then fell silent a few moments. "We're trying to figure out what to do with it when I retire and after we die."

"Die? Neither of you are dying. You can toss that thought right out of your head."

"Any of us could go at any time. I've got to get prepared, and I don't love the options. You're doing well with your research. David's busy with his medical practice, and Hannah's set on teaching."

They climbed the steps and entered the mudroom. Taking off his boots and outerwear, Michael tried to control the anxiety his dad's words brought up. He'd been going from research job to research job for years, and he'd given little thought to his own future all that time. Worse, he'd taken for granted the fact that his parents and the ranch would always be here for him to return to.

"I smell snickerdoodles. Come on." Dad grinned and entered the kitchen. Michael followed.

Hannah, wearing an apron over her sweater and holding a spatula in one hand, squealed. "You're here!"

"Didn't we already go through this last night?" Michael hugged her, lifting her off her toes. "Did you think I'd vanish into thin air?"

"No, but I've been missing you." She punched his arm. "I can't remember the last time I saw you for more than a day or two. And now we get you for two whole weeks." Her wheat-blond hair wrapped over her shoulder in a long braid. "We're doing all the traditions. The Christmas parade. Watching movies. Oh, and the children's nativity play..."

"I'm with Hannah on this." His mom beamed. "I'm glad you're home, honey."

After kissing his mother's cheek, he grabbed three cookies—still warm—and shoveled one into his mouth.

"Where did you run off to this morning, anyway?" Hannah popped a fist on one hip and narrowed her eyes at him.

"Just checked on Leann's car and stopped in at Dandy's to see if she and her daughter were all right."

"And are they?" Hannah asked.

"Yeah. John Fulton's going to tow her car to his shop later." He frowned. "And Leann seems okay, except for her arm. She must have injured it in the accident."

"That does it." His mom placed a sheet of cookies in the oven before straightening. "She needs to come out to the ranch. She and her little girl can stay here. If this woman's arm is injured, she's going to have a terrible time taking care of a toddler."

"Ma..." He rolled his eyes. His mother took personal responsibility for every hurt thing she encountered, whether it was an owl, coyote or human.

"Don't roll your eyes at me, Michael Lee Carr." She pointed her finger at him. "I'm right and you know it."

"She isn't going to agree to stay here. She doesn't know us. Well, I guess she knows Kelli."

"Oh, she's the one Kelli hired to manage the store?" Hannah's face brightened. "I've been looking forward to meeting her."

"Yes." He knew he sounded like a bear and didn't care. "She should stay with Kelli. They have a house full of kids for Sunni to play with." Even as he said it, he wanted to take the words back. He didn't like the thought of Leann staying with his brother.

"She couldn't possibly stay with David and Kelli." Mom shook her head. "Their house is chaos right now. Between their busy jobs and dealing with the baby's colic, it's a wonder those two are functioning at all. Which reminds me, Hannah, David called while you were in the shower to ask if you could work the reception desk for Dixie at the clinic after lunch. Her daughter has the flu."

"Of course. I'm happy to help." Hannah resumed scooping dough onto cookie sheets.

"Have you seen your brother yet?" Mom watched him expectantly.

"No." He wasn't getting into this with her. His mom's feelings were clear about his and David's estrangement. She wanted them to be best friends—close, like the way they'd been when they were kids. How was he supposed to be close to the man who'd stolen the woman he'd loved?

It wasn't going to happen.

"It's Christmas," Mom said. "The season of hope. Don't you think it's time to forgive and move on?"

He clenched his jaw. Easy for her to say. David had never even apologized.

Although Michael hadn't dated Kelli long, he'd fallen for her hard. She'd been exciting, fun. Then he'd accepted a three-month research assignment in Montana. His feelings for her had grown stronger while they were apart, so strong he'd considered proposing when he'd returned to Sunrise Bend. But he hadn't known her feelings had cooled or that she'd gotten close to his own brother.

David had stolen her from Michael.

And after six years, Michael still couldn't forgive him. He doubted he ever would.

Chapter Three

❦

"Is everyone able to get into the clinic so quickly?" Leann strolled next to Michael on the sidewalk leading to the entry. The rush of anticipation when he'd pulled up to the B and B in his truck this afternoon had brought her back to high school infatuations. Silly, really. She glanced his way. He carried Sunni, who was blowing kisses to the world.

"I have connections." He opened the door for her, and she stomped the snow off her boots before approaching the front desk.

"Hey, Michael!" The pretty receptionist lit up when she saw him.

Jealousy pinched Leann's heart. *Really, Leann?* She had no claim on the man.

"Hannah, this is Leann Bowden and her daughter, Sunni. Leann, my sister, Hannah."

His *sister*? She could handle that. The muscles in her shoulders relaxed.

"It's great to meet you," Leann said.

"You, too. Once you fill these out, we'll get you right in." Hannah grinned and handed her a clipboard with forms attached. Then she turned to Michael. "Do you want me to tell David you're here?"

Leann sensed his body stiffen.

"No, thanks."

She glanced up at him and was surprised at the hardness in his face. He set Sunni down and turned to Leann. "I'm going to run over to the auto shop and see if John's had a chance to tow your car. I'll be back soon." He nodded to her and Hannah, then left.

Leann furrowed her eyebrows as the door shut behind him. He was acting weird.

"Where Myco go?" Sunni tugged on Leann's coat.

"He'll be right back, sweetheart." She found a seat and helped Sunni onto the chair next to her. Several minutes later, after filling out the necessary forms, Leann held Sunni's hand as a nurse led them to an examination room.

Hannah peeked in. "Hey, do you want me to watch Sunni for you while you talk to my brother?"

Her brother? Michael couldn't be back already, could he? And why would he be allowed back here?

"Hannah, how many times have I told you to call me Dr. Carr when you're at the clinic?" A tall, dark-haired man with mischievous eyes walked in and held out his hand. "Dr. David Carr. How can I help you?"

"Oh!" It finally hit her—this was Kelli's husband. Which meant…Michael was…his brother? Michael hadn't mentioned his last name. Leann tried to recall Kelli discussing her husband's family, but nothing came up. "It's nice to meet you. So…the three of you are siblings?" She pointed to Hannah and back to him.

"The three of us?" He frowned.

"Michael found Leann and Sunni trapped in the storm last night," Hannah said. "Her car slid off the road."

"Wait, you're Leann? Kelli has been talking my ear off about how you're going to manage the store. I'm her husband. It's good to finally meet you." He pumped her good hand. He seemed genuinely happy to meet her, which was a relief.

"Same to you. I can't wait to see Kelli. I'm excited to start working for her." She pointed to him then Hannah. "Do you have other brothers and sisters I should know about before I stick my foot in my mouth around town?"

"No, just us three." Hannah chuckled.

David's expression faltered, but he recovered quickly. "What seems to be the problem today?"

"Come on, Sunni, let's find the stickers." Hannah held out her hand. With questions in her eyes, Sunni stared up at Leann.

"It's okay. You can go with Hannah. This will only take a few minutes. The doctor's going to help my arm."

"Mama, boo-boo?"

"Yep."

Sunni gave her a long backward stare as Hannah, happily chattering about candy canes and puppy stickers, steered her to the hall.

Leann turned her attention back to David. "Please tell Kelli I'll come over to the store to see her as soon as I can. I tried calling her earlier."

"I'll tell her, but don't worry about it. With all the snow, she didn't open The Sassy Lasso today." He began examining her arm. "The baby was up half the night with colic, and he's been wearing us both out. I turned her phone to Silent so she could get some sleep."

"Colic? Ouch. I'm sorry. Babies are hard enough when they aren't colicky. Is there anything I can do to help?"

"You managing the store after the holidays will be a tremendous help. We're thankful you're moving here." David chatted about Kelli and their three kids as he continued his examination, and Leann relaxed. He was charming and seemed nice.

"Well, I have good news and bad news. You pulled a muscle in your shoulder. It should heal quickly. The wrist, though, is a moderate sprain. You'll need to wear a splint for ten days…" He discussed resting it, applying ice and taking medication to alleviate the pain and swelling. "We have splints here. Hannah will get you the right size. Any questions?"

"Obviously carrying Sunni is off-limits, right?"

"Carrying anything is off-limits."

Exactly what she'd feared. How was she going to take care of Sunni with all those stairs at the bed-and-breakfast? Leann stood. "Thank you for seeing me on such short notice."

"You're welcome. You and Sunni should come to the nativity play at church Sunday night. We're having a small party afterward at our house. We'd like it if you joined us."

"Thank you. We'd love that."

"See you then." He shook her hand again and left the room.

Michael's family sure was welcoming. Was something off between David and Michael, though? Or was she reading into things? Wouldn't be the first time. It wasn't any of her business, anyhow.

Hannah brought Sunni back into the room.

"Mama!" Sunni held up two fistfuls of stickers.

"Oh, wow. You are loaded up." She turned to Hannah. "Thank you for watching her."

"She's a doll. Mom and I were talking this morning, and we would love for you and Sunni to stay with us at the ranch—at least until you're 100 percent again." She gestured to Leann's wrist. "My mom is all about spoiling babies, and the house is huge. You'd have your privacy."

"I don't know." Leann bit her lower lip. "It's very kind of you, but…"

"Just think about it. I'll find you a splint."

"I will."

Hannah's invitation tempted her. But this was Michael's family, not hers. From what she'd seen of the Carrs, they all seemed nice, but she didn't know them. And she didn't want to make Michael uncomfortable. He was supposed to be enjoying Christmas vacation with his parents and sister. Imposing on them felt wrong. But staying with his welcoming family at Christmastime sure was tempting… and it was kind of them to ask.

"Your car won't be ready until after Christmas." Michael boosted Sunni into her car seat and buckled her in as Leann settled into the passenger side of his truck.

"At least another week then, huh?" She bit her lower lip. "Today's Thursday, and Christmas Eve is next Wednesday…"

"Yeah, I don't see your car being done before then." Michael got into the driver's seat and cast her a glance. It had been simple to avoid his brother at the clinic, but instead of relief, he had mixed feelings. The last time he'd seen David was a year ago, and besides *Merry Christmas* they hadn't spoken a word to each other. "So, what's the verdict?"

"My wrist is sprained." She lifted it, stiff from the splint under her coat, and shot him a resigned look.

"Let me guess. You need to rest it."

"Yep. I have to ice it for the next couple of days and avoid any pressure on it for at least a week."

He fired the engine. Resting her arm wouldn't be easy with Sunni around. His mom's and sister's suggestion for Leann and Sunni to stay at the ranch came to mind. It was on the tip of his tongue to invite her, but it wouldn't be wise. He couldn't deny his attraction, and the feeling wouldn't be mutual. Even if it was, he'd be leaving soon.

But…she was hurt and she did need help.

"Why didn't you tell me the doctor was your brother?"

"I figured you knew. You're Kelli's friend." Now that she'd met his handsome, successful older brother, Michael was probably a distant second in her eyes. It was what had happened with Kelli. Not that Leann would be thinking about either of them.

"I wasn't very close with Kelli." She glanced at him. "We ran around with the same friends in college. She was a year older than me. We didn't keep in touch after we graduated, but our mutual friend Janelle talks to her regularly. Janelle's the one who told me about the job."

"Ah." He hadn't realized she wasn't best friends with his ex-girlfriend, now sister-in-law. The thought warmed him more than the blast of heat from the truck's console. "What did you have planned today?"

"Well, I was going to stop over at The Sassy Lasso to say hello to Kelli and to get a feel for the store, but David said she didn't open it today. So…I don't have any plans. What about you?"

"I'm on Christmas break." He drove out of the parking lot. "No plans for me beyond checking cattle with Dad."

"Now that my car has been taken care of and my arm is all set, please don't feel obligated to help anymore. You don't have to take care of me."

Take care of her? He checked his rearview. Sunni was happily staring out the window. Then he peeked at Leann. Her quiet strength told him she'd been taking care of herself for a long time.

No one else was taking care of her or her daughter.

And maybe it wasn't the smartest move, but he couldn't resist filling the role. He wanted to help her.

At least for now.

"I don't mind." He gestured to her. "Why don't you come out to the ranch for a while? Sunni might like to see the dogs and barn cats. They're all friendly."

"I'd like that." She smiled at him. With her long dark brown hair and big blue eyes, she was striking. More than striking. Beautiful.

Not trusting himself to speak, he nodded and steered the truck toward his parents' ranch. The rolling, snow-covered countryside whizzed by as he drove. He knew every inch of this route. The years he'd been gone hadn't erased the memories of home. He found it reassuring.

This piece of Wyoming was part of him.

"I never asked where you're from." He peeked at Leann.

"St. Louis. Born and raised."

"You'll be missing your family, then, at Christmas."

"No, I'm afraid I won't. My grandmother raised me, but she passed a long time ago. It's one of the reasons I'm looking forward to living here. I figure it will be easier to meet people in a small town..."

He enjoyed listening to her talk about creating new memories here for Sunni and how she was determined to make this Christmas wonderful. He didn't say it, but he couldn't help thinking it would be hard to create Christmas memories at the bed-and-breakfast. Soon the driveway with the Carr Ranch sign hanging between two log posts appeared. "Here we are."

The cattle were foraging in the distant pasture. The cold didn't bother them; they looked content. He wondered if he should check fence in the other pastures tomorrow. Yesterday's snow might have damaged them. He'd mention it to Dad later. After parking the truck, he helped Leann down and got Sunni out of her car seat. She snuggled into his arms as if she belonged there.

"Where we at, Myco?" She pointed to the large log home, decorated with evergreen boughs, red ribbons and white lights.

"This is where my parents live." With one hand on Leann's arm and the other carrying Sunni, he made sure they both safely got to the front entrance.

He set the child down and helped her unzip her coat then pointed to the hall closet. "You can hang your coat there, Leann."

She crossed to the closet while he helped Sunni take off her boots.

"Come on—I'll introduce you to my mom." He gestured for them to follow him. Sunni sidled next to his leg as he entered the kitchen.

His mom was stirring something on the stove. She grinned when she saw them. "You must be Leann. I'm Patty, Michael's mother. Did he convince you to stay with us yet?"

"Ma-a-a…" He widened his eyes, but his mother shooed him.

"Well, actually Hannah mentioned it, but…" Leann blushed.

"We'd love to have you." His mom pointed to the splint on her wrist. "We can't have you staying at the B and B with that arm. It's no way to spend the holidays."

"I couldn't…"

"Of course you could." She beamed.

"But I'd be imposing."

"Imposing? Oh, honey, you couldn't if you tried. We love a full house. It's been so dull and quiet here—the empty nest is not my thing." Patty noticed Sunni. "Well, how did I miss you, cutie pie? What's your name?"

Sunni wrapped her arms around Michael's leg and stared, wide-eyed, up at his mom.

"It's okay, Sunni." He bent down and picked her up. "This is my mom. She'll give you cookies."

"Cookie." Sunni brightened.

"Come here, sugar." His mom held out her arms, and Sunni readily went to her. "Aren't you the prettiest little thing? Did Michael tell you we have doggies and kitties in the barn? And I'm guessing we have a room here with your name on it."

"Kitty?"

"Yes, ma'am." Patty tapped her finger on the end of Sunni's nose.

His concerns about Leann staying here were selfish. How could he deprive her of the opportunity to heal her wrist? Not to mention his mom would love to spoil Sunni.

Michael arched his eyebrows at Leann. "What do you think? Do you and Sunni want to stay here?"

His mom shifted Sunni to her hip and pointed at Leann's splint. "You need help until the brace is off. Frank and I will set up a room for you."

Leann looked shell-shocked, so he guided her to the living room.

"I know my mom comes on strong, but she's right. It would be easier on you if you stayed here. We'll all help with Sunni."

"I'm not sure about this." She chewed on her bottom lip. "I don't know your family. I think I can manage okay at the B and B."

"Just think about it. I'll drive you into town or wherever you need to go while you're here. And you'd have your own room. You don't need to spend every minute with us."

"It's very nice of you to offer, but…"

"You don't have to explain." He caught the longing in her expression. "For what it's worth, though, it would make my mom and Hannah happy."

"What about you?" She lifted shy eyes to him.

"It would make me happy, too."

Her lips curved into a nervous smile. "Then, yes, I'm grateful for your offer. I'll stay. But if it's too much, I'll go right back to the B and B. Honestly, I don't mind."

Anticipation added a spring to his pulse. "Why don't we show Sunni the dogs and cats, then we'll go back to town to get your bags."

"If we show Sunni the dogs and cats, you'll never get us to leave."

He had to look away from her glowing face. Was it a good thing or a bad thing that the single mom and her cute toddler were staying at the ranch? Either way, something told him it would be a Christmas to remember.

Chapter Four

❧

"Squeeze the frosting on like this." The next day after lunch, Leann helped Sunni hold a pastry bag filled with red frosting. They'd staked out their decorating position on a stool at the kitchen counter. Hannah and Patty were whipping up batches of colored frostings and setting out bowls full of assorted sprinkles. Happy Christmas music filled the air. Leann enjoyed listening to Patty banter with Hannah. And, if she were being honest, she envied their relationship a teensy bit.

What would it be like to be part of such a loving family?

Leann thought about her conversation with Michael about family yesterday. She missed her grandmother. Even growing up, she'd never had a big family Christmas, but now that she was around Patty and Hannah, she understood the appeal. Thinking about how she'd celebrated the previous two holidays—just her and Sunni—brought an ache to her heart. They'd been lonely.

"I'm going to pop in to David's this afternoon and give the babysitter a break from Owen's crying. Poor Genevieve is probably praising the good Lord it's Friday so she'll have the weekend off from all his screaming. Besides, I need to deliver these cookies to them for Sunday's party."

Patty spread wax paper onto the counter. She stood a few inches over five feet, and she kept her chestnut hair short with fluffed soft curls. Her striped green-and-red sweater skimmed the pockets of her jeans. If Leann could choose the perfect grandmother for Sunni, Patty would be it.

"Do you think Rachel and Bobby will be there?" Hannah asked her mom. Then she turned to Leann. "They're Kelli and David's older children, although four and two can hardly be called old."

Patty shook her head. "I thought David said they were having a playdate with the Johnson kids."

"Too bad. I told Rachel we could watch *Frosty the Snowman* together soon." Hannah momentarily paused from scooping purple frosting into a pastry bag. "You don't think she's too young to watch it, do you?"

"She'll bawl her eyes out when Frosty melts, regardless, Hannah. Doesn't matter how old she is."

Leann always got teary at that part, too. Sunni squirted a big blob of frosting on the wax paper. Leann grabbed the bag. "Whoops, let's try to keep it on the cookie." She kissed the top of Sunni's head.

Hannah finished with the purple frosting, wiped her hands on a towel and typed on her phone. "I might as well ask Kelli when would be a good time."

"Do you know if Kelli will be at the store today?" Leann asked. Her new boss still hadn't returned her calls. Granted, Leann had only been in town for a full day, there had been a massive snowstorm and the woman was dealing with a challenging baby, but still…

"Oh, yes. Not much keeps her away from her pride and joy." Patty set freshly baked cutout cookies on the wax paper. "I'm glad she hired you. She's been running herself ragged between the boutique and those three little ones. We help as much as possible, but…"

"Well, Kelli likes to do things herself." Hannah set her phone back on the counter before adding yellow food coloring to a bowl of white icing. "And there's nothing wrong with that. She's a great mom, and her store is a hit."

Leann sensed the *but*.

"I hope she isn't being unrealistic about suddenly becoming a stay-at-home mom. Oh, no!" Patty smacked her forehead. "I forgot the cinnamon candies. Hannah, remind me to tell Frank to pick them up later."

"What's this I need to pick up?" Frank entered the room. His face was ruddy from the cold, and he wore a flannel shirt with jeans. Michael padded in behind him, looking rugged and very attractive. Too attractive. Leann averted her gaze as her heartbeat pounded.

"The Red Hots candies. I can't believe I forgot them."

"Hi there, Sunni." Frank scrunched his nose, grinned and waved. She bounced in excitement on Leann's lap and held up a cookie smeared with frosting that had about a pound of sprinkles jammed on top. He pretended to take a bite. "You always forget them."

"I do not!" Patty planted both hands on her hips.

"You do, and you know it. Every year it's the same thing. Those Red Hots cinnamon candies. And a few days later it's the chocolate Kisses." He shook his head, clearly enjoying himself. "Am I right, Hannah, or am I right?"

"Don't drag me into this." Hannah thrust her palms out in front of her. Then she cupped her hand and whispered to Leann, "He's right."

Leann tucked her lips under to keep from laughing. Their teasing came so naturally. What would it be like to banter with a husband like Patty did with Frank? She sneaked a peek at Michael and instantly regretted it.

He was off-limits.

As if reading her mind, Michael came over and sat on the stool next to her.

"Myco!" Sunni shoved the cookie toward him.

"Ooh, that looks good. Can I decorate one, too?" He pointed to the plain cookies on the plate in front of her. She nodded.

"How about a—" he poked his chin around to look at them all "—wreath?"

"See doggies?" She pointed to the door.

"You liked them, didn't you? Let's decorate the cookies first. We'll see the dogs later, okay?"

"'Kay!"

Leann's heart grew mushy. Michael was so good with Sunni. If he lived in Sunrise Bend…

But he didn't, and she had to stop fantasizing that he would.

Patty lined up pastry bags with different colors of frosting. "There. If you'll all help, we should be able to knock out these cookies by this afternoon. Michael, you can help me take them to David's later. They're for the party Sunday."

Leann sneaked a peek at him. His jaw tightened, and he didn't say a word.

Her cell phone rang.

"I'll take Sunni so you can answer it." Michael hauled her daughter onto his lap.

"Thanks." Leann excused herself and padded down the hallway to the staircase leading up to the guest rooms. "Hello?"

"Hey, Leann." Kelli sounded chipper through the line. "Sorry I haven't gotten back to you. Things have been crazy here."

"I understand."

"David told me about your wrist. How awful! Are you doing okay?"

"Yes, I'm actually staying with his parents at the ranch."

"Oh." The line was silent for two beats. "That's... thoughtful of them. Can you come into town later? I'd like to show you around the store."

"Sure. I'll ask Michael to take me."

"Michael?" She sounded confused. "Don't you have a car?"

"It's in the shop. It got pretty banged up in the accident."

"I see." Silence stretched. "Well, this is my cell phone, so text me when you're on your way."

"I will. I'm looking forward to seeing you."

Kelli hung up.

Was she imagining it or had there been a lot of strange undercurrents in the conversation?

She returned to the kitchen and sat next to Michael with Sunni on his lap.

"That was Kelli. She wants me to come to the store this afternoon. Would you mind dropping me off?"

"Not at all." The words were tighter than a ball of rubber bands.

Was she imagining the tension? She'd have to be blind not to notice every time David was mentioned Michael clammed up. But did the problem extend to Kelli, as well?

Exactly what was going on between them?

"When are you picking up Leann?" Michael's dad asked. Hannah had volunteered to watch Sunni while Leann spent a few hours at The Sassy Lasso with Kelli. Michael had dropped Leann off twenty minutes ago, driven back to the ranch and joined his dad to do chores. He certainly wasn't sticking around the store to see his ex-girlfriend.

"I have to leave in an hour and a half."

"Plenty of time. Let's load the hay for tomorrow."

Michael followed his dad to the barn and began tossing bales onto the hay sleigh. Whenever the snow was thick, his dad hitched a team of horses and dragged the hay out to the cattle each day. Michael had always loved joining him. There was something majestic about a rolling, snow-covered prairie, blue skies and the silence of winter.

"You're still strong." Dad wiped his forehead with the back of his glove. "I wasn't sure how much physical labor you were doing up there in Canada."

"Yeah, the research part doesn't build muscle." He missed these easy conversations with Dad. "Chopping wood and hauling supplies does, though."

His dad chuckled. "When you taking off again?"

"I don't know." He grew serious. "Jan is going to Alaska to study Arctic grayling fish. She wants me to join her and her crew."

"But you haven't said yes? I'm surprised."

"Honestly, I am, too. I'm not sure why I've been on the fence about it."

"Take your time deciding." Dad nodded. "Stay here as long as you'd like."

Michael tossed several more hay bales onto the sleigh. His forearms and biceps began to burn from the exertion. He liked ranching. Enjoyed hard, physical labor. But ever since he'd left Sunrise Bend to pursue a career studying wildlife, he hadn't looked back. Well, not seriously, at least.

"You know, David's changed some." Dad pulled bales of hay off the stacks and dragged them over. "Kelli has, too. They're both more grounded."

He wasn't having this conversation. If Dad thought Michael was going to make things right with David when his brother was the one in the wrong, he was going to be disappointed. With more force than necessary, Michael threw a bale on top of the pile. It bounced and fell off the other side. He jogged over and set it on top, then returned.

"It's been six years, son."

"I know." Like he didn't know how long it had been. When Michael had met Kelli, he'd been dazzled by her bright, energetic personality. He'd had no clue why she'd been willing to date him when she could have been with any other guy—a more interesting, exciting one. And he hadn't cared, because she'd liked him. For a while, at least.

"Are you over her?" Dad asked.

He opened his mouth to answer, but nothing came out. Was he over Kelli? It wasn't something he'd really considered. In fact, whenever she or David invaded his thoughts, he pushed them away and refused to dwell on them.

"I don't know," he answered truthfully. But as soon as he said it, he wondered if he'd been lying to himself all along. He didn't miss Kelli. He missed his brother. "Coming home and finding out she and David were a couple... I mean, I asked him to watch out for her. I didn't expect him to poach my girlfriend."

"Don't you think Kelli had some part in it, too?"

He hadn't spoken about this with anyone. Ever. It was too humiliating. Dad might want to discuss it at length, but Michael would rather pretend it had never happened.

And how's that been working out for you?

"I reckon Kelli was at fault, too." Michael propped a boot onto a hay bale and looked his father in the eye. It didn't take a genius to figure out she had completely forgotten about him in the three short months he'd been in Montana.

"Maybe your brother did you a favor."

"What?" Michael set his boot back on the ground and widened his stance.

"Now that I've gotten to know Kelli, I don't think she would have been a good match for you, son. She's go-go-go. And you're quieter, more inclined to think long and hard before you make decisions."

Great. Even his dad thought he was boring.

"I like Kelli. Respect her. I'm glad she's part of our family, but she and David are compatible." Dad resumed hauling the hay bales off the stack. "Take Leann in there. She strikes me as the kind of woman who'd appreciate a man like you."

His heart pounded like galloping hooves on the prairie. It shouldn't have surprised him, but it did. He had no business getting all nerved up for a woman he'd known less than two days.

But he couldn't help wondering if Dad was right. Could a woman like Leann be interested in a guy like him?

"It wouldn't work. When I leave for six months on a research trip? I don't see a nice woman like her waiting around. She's got a kid to raise."

"Maybe you're not giving her enough credit. People in the military leave spouses behind all the time. I guess you'll have to ask yourself what you want. If you want to get married and start a family, you might have to put the research jobs on hold for a while."

"For a while? Try forever."

His dad let out a throaty laugh. "Forever? You're as dramatic as your sister. Twenty years flies by in a blink of an eye. Take me. I feel like it was yesterday when I carried your mother over the threshold. Then I blinked and found out I was going to be a dad. And didn't we just buy you kids those puppies for Christmas?"

"I loved those border collies." Michael chuckled. "Boots was my best friend when I was eight."

"I know. And now look at you all—grown up with lives of your own. Life goes quick. Just think about what I said."

His dad had been awfully talkative today. Maybe he was right. Maybe avoiding the subject for six years hadn't helped him move on. His relationship with David was still nonexistent, and he hadn't taken a chance with a woman since he'd dated Kelli.

Michael tossed the final bale of hay on the sleigh. Was he really willing to live alone and isolated indefinitely?

Chapter Five

❧

"Wow, Kelli, you've outdone yourself. The cowboy-boot selection is to die for." Leann trailed her fingers along the tips of the women's cowboy boots lovingly spotlighted along a wall.

"Thanks." Kelli's wavy blond hair bounced as she strode to a rack of shirts. Thin but curvy, she had a take-charge personality and an infectious smile. She looked too impossibly put-together to have three small children and a thriving business. "Every year I try to shake things up a little. I change the color palette of the accessories and try new purse styles. We're always rotating in new jewelry and clothing. You don't think the chandeliers are too much, do you?"

"No, not at all." Leann craned her neck back to take in the sparkling light fixtures. "They give it an upscale but friendly air. I'm surprised you can get anyone to leave. I'd want to shop in here all day."

"The way the baby is carrying on, *I* want to shop in here all day." Kelli shot her a look of long-suffering before striding to the back room.

"I'm sorry he's fussy." Leann followed her. Rows of shelves, all tagged with pretty handmade signs, held the store's inventory. The door to an office was open. She peeked inside. A gleaming white desk, pale pink walls, a laptop and a fluffy pink rug filled the small space.

Leann could see herself working here. The store was everything she'd imagined and more. She wanted to hug herself. The only concern she had was adjusting to working full-time after only working part-time for so long.

"*Fussy* doesn't describe it. The pediatrician said most babies get over colic around three months, but Owen's almost five months old, and he isn't letting up. We've tried switching his formula, giving him soothing massages, using essential oils, you name it. The baby is miserable. And so am I. It's brutal, Leann."

She murmured her sympathy. *Thank You, Lord, for sparing Sunni from having colic.* Leann didn't think she could have handled that on top of the divorce so soon after her daughter's birth.

"This is the one time being married to a doctor isn't helping. David is out of ideas. I wish there were a cure-all. I'd try anything." Kelli stopped and pressed her hand against a rack of shoe boxes.

"Are you okay?" Leann asked, lightly touching Kelli's shoulder.

"I'm fine." She straightened, giving her a tight smile. "As you can see, there's a lot of inventory to deal with. It might take some time for you to get the hang of it here."

"You're very organized, and I'm a fast learner."

"I'm sure you are, but it might be smart for me to stay on as manager through the spring."

Wait. What? Why would Kelli want to keep working after the holidays?

Leann held her chin high. "I worked as a retail manager for three years before having Sunni, and I've been an assistant manager for the past two. I'm up to the challenge."

"I know. But this is a big undertaking." A shadow crossed over her face. For the first time, Leann noticed the dark circles under her eyes.

"You don't have to worry about me managing the store, Kelli."

Kelli continued forward. "So you're getting to know Michael?"

What a strange question. "He's been helping me get my car fixed and basic stuff like carrying Sunni since my wrist is sprained."

"Why him?" The words sounded nonchalant, but the hair on Leann's arms rose.

"Well, he's the one who found us. My car slid off the road right into the Welcome to Sunrise Bend sign on our way into town. Sunni and I were trapped there for hours in the cold."

"David told me something to that effect. Michael to the rescue," Kelli muttered, waving her into the office. "I suppose you know all about it, then."

"About what?" What in the world was going on between the brothers?

"Oh, spare me the feigned innocence. I'm sure you think I'm a terrible person. But, honestly, the years of silence are not my fault. That's on David and Michael. The family can't pin *everything* on me."

"What are you talking about?" Anxiety started building in Leann's gut. She needed this job, and she needed to get along well with Kelli. If there was a problem between the Carrs and her boss, it wouldn't look good for Leann to be staying with them. This conversation wasn't reassuring her.

"Michael and I dated years ago. I'd just moved here and leased this building. I liked him, but he left after a couple of months to go study minnows or something. And David came back to town to work at the clinic."

Leann tried not to cringe as she began to piece it together.

"What can I say?" Kelli shrugged. "David has a dynamic personality. And Michael was...gone."

It was on the tip of Leann's tongue to say Michael had a great personality, too. But she couldn't argue with gone.

Her ex-husband, Luke, hadn't stuck around, either.

"I didn't mean to fall in love with David. It just happened. And I made the right choice. Michael is always away on research projects. We never would have worked. You can't exactly build a relationship with someone who lives in the wilderness for years." Kelli spun away and picked up a pen. "So now you know. Let me walk you through my vision for the next quarter..."

Leann thought back on what Michael had told her. He'd said he wasn't sure where he'd be going next. There was the possibility he'd move to Alaska, or anywhere in the world, for that matter. She hadn't fully realized what a nomadic life he lived.

The niggling worry from earlier grew stronger. Kelli wasn't making her feel secure about her new job in her new town. And it didn't help to know the man Leann was attracted to had not only dated her boss but moved constantly.

She thought of the tension she'd picked up on over the past few days.

Was Michael still in love with Kelli?

She'd have to think about it later. For now, she needed to soak in everything Kelli told her about the store.

"How did it go?" Michael ambled next to Leann on the sidewalks of Main Street later that afternoon. He'd waited outside The Sassy Lasso while she'd finished up.

"Good… I think." She seemed bothered by something.

"Want to grab a cup of coffee before we head back?"

"Sure." She shoved her hands into the pockets of her wool coat. "Oh, but Hannah's already been watching Sunni for so long."

"When I left, Sunni had fallen asleep on the couch. Want me to text Hannah and see if she's still sleeping?"

"Yes, please." Her grateful smile sent a burst of warmth through his chest.

He texted Hannah, and her reply came instantly.

Still sleeping. He pointed down the street. "Morning Brew has a good selection of coffee."

"Sounds great."

As they strolled along, Leann stopped to view the festive shop windows and raved about the decorative details. He enjoyed seeing the town through her eyes. It had been years since he'd taken an unrushed stroll through town. He was glad to do it on a winter's day with Leann.

"Whoever did this one should be proud of themselves," she said. "Making gingerbread houses so perfectly takes talent. See the delicate latticework on the porch? Amazing."

"You notice things other people skim over."

"You think so?" She slipped on an icy patch. He held out his hand to steady her, and she grabbed his arm. Her simple touch sent heat through his body. "Thank you."

They reached the coffee shop, and he held the door open for her. After ordering a decaf mochaccino for Leann and an espresso for himself, they found a small table in the corner near a Christmas tree. The place was decorated with stuffed moose, bears, white twinkle lights and red flannel bows.

Sitting across from him, Leann looked prettier than any model in a magazine, but her forehead wrinkled as if she had something on her mind. Then she shook her head slightly. "Tell me about the research you do."

She wanted to know about his research? Not many people asked about it, but he wasn't around all that many people, either. Maybe she was being polite.

"Last year I was on a team studying the size and coloration of various trout populations. Based on our data, we determined which ones were at risk. We also came up with recovery strategies." As the words streamed out of his mouth, his heart sank. Who besides his colleagues wanted to hear about trout populations? The topic was sure to bore her.

"Really?" Her eyes lit with interest. "Were you outside a lot? What does a typical day look like for you?"

Did she really want to know more? Or was she being polite?

"We're outside most of the time." He toyed with the handle of his cup of espresso. "When we're not outdoors studying the fish, we spend hours creating reports in our cabins."

"A lot of work. Tell me about the fish. Trout, right?"

He blinked. She wanted to hear about the trout? He got the impression she truly was interested—she didn't seem bored in the slightest. He explained his research methods and what he looked for, and as the conversation went on, he opened up more and more.

"You love your job, don't you?" She took the final sip of her coffee.

"Most of the time." He grew serious. "It has its drawbacks, though."

"Like what?"

"I move from place to place every six months to a year, depending on the research grants. I don't have a home base, not one of my own, at least. The hours are long and sporadic, and I take vacations between projects. Since I don't have an employer, I don't have benefits. It gets lonely."

"But you don't work alone."

"No, I don't. I've been fortunate to pair up with my research partner, Jan, for several projects." He didn't always see eye to eye with Jan, but he respected her tenacity and dedication to wildlife.

"I guess it means you'll be heading to Alaska soon." She averted her gaze.

"I'm not sure, yet." Studying the Arctic grayling fish would boost his professional reputation. But he thought about his dad and the ranch. How much he was enjoying checking cattle and riding horseback for a good part of the day. "When do you start at The Sassy Lasso?"

"January third." She traced the rim of her mug. "I need this job. I'm not desperate or anything—my ex-husband, Luke, pays generous child support and I have a little savings. Don't get me wrong—I need at least a part-time job, but when I heard about managing the boutique, well, I got excited for the first time in a long time. I like the fact that it's not a franchise and I'd have more responsibility. I don't know if that makes sense."

"I get it. Growing up, I always thought I'd join my dad in ranching, but my junior year of high school, I spent a summer volunteering with the Wyoming Game and Fish Department. I was hooked—pardon the pun."

She chuckled, and it sent a ripple of sensation over his skin. She made him feel like he wasn't as boring as he thought.

"You gave up ranching, huh?" she asked.

"I did. It was a hard decision, but I decided to go to college to become a wildlife researcher. When you say you need the job—for you—I get it. Becoming a wildlife researcher was something I needed, too." He rarely opened up like this with anyone. And saying it out loud brought questions to mind. Like did he still need it? Was he taking research jobs out of habit? "Anyway, you'll make a great manager."

"You think so?" The hope in her tone soon gave way to a sigh. "Kelli hinted it might take me some time to get the hang of how the store is run. She might stay on as manager for a while after the holidays."

It was on the tip of his tongue to warn her not to rely on Kelli, but just because his sister-in-law had played him false didn't mean she couldn't be trusted. He wouldn't feel right speaking ill of her.

"I need to find an apartment." Leann met his gaze. "Any suggestions?"

He noted the worry lines between her eyebrows. If he was on speaking terms with Kelli, he'd be blunt and tell her to stop yanking Leann around. But he wasn't on speaking terms, and he didn't plan to be anytime soon.

"Well, I haven't lived here in years, but not much changes in Sunrise Bend. There's an apartment complex on the east side of town. That would be your best option. Some of the stores here on Main Street have apartments above them, too. I'll have my mom put out the word that you're looking for an apartment. She's always on top of local happenings."

"Thanks. I already spoke with the two day-care centers here, and they both have spots for Sunni. I'll stop in and check them out before deciding, but it can wait until after Christmas."

"Name the time. I'll drive you over."

"Thanks."

They sat in easy silence, soaking in the instrumental Christmas music.

"Michael?"

"Hmm?"

"Kelli told me what happened," Leann said. "I didn't know you two had dated before she married David. She told me this afternoon."

"No big deal. Why would you know?" He rapped his knuckles on the tabletop. He was partly relieved she hadn't known and partly mortified she did now.

"I'm sorry." She covered his hand with hers. Her gentle touch didn't soothe the emotions her words had kicked up.

"Are you ready to go?" He pulled his hand back. "Need to stop anywhere?"

She took the abrupt change of topic in stride. "Most of Sunni's presents are still in the trunk of my car. I didn't buy much. She had a birthday last month, and I don't want to spoil her."

"Let's stop at the auto shop and get the presents out of the trunk." He rose and took their empty cups. "Then we can go to Lindy Loo's General Store."

"Lindy Loo's?"

"Yep." He set the dishes in the tub on top of the trash receptacle and waited for Leann to button her coat. A text came through from his mom. He read it and pocketed his phone. "I guess that decides it. Mom just texted me. She needs her cinnamon candies. Lindy Loo's, it is."

Leann slid her gloves on as he opened the door. "Does this Lindy Loo's carry toys?"

"It's a variety store. You can find anything there."

"Anything, huh? I'll pick up a few last-minute items for Sunni while you grab the candy."

He was glad she'd taken the hint and dropped the topic of him and Kelli. It had been years ago. They all just needed to let it go.

But if he was still avoiding his brother and couldn't bring himself to step inside Kelli's store, had he really let it go?

Chapter Six

"Look, Sunni, there's a sucker!" Leann pointed to the candy tossed in their direction Saturday morning. They stood on the sidewalk in front of an insurance agency. The sun was out for the annual Christmas parade, and infectious joy filled the air. Leann closed her eyes for the briefest moment to savor the blessing of giving her daughter the happiest of Christmas seasons. They were already creating memories and traditions in their new town.

Sunni stretched forward to grasp the sucker in her mitten-covered hand.

"Where's my sucker?" Michael asked Sunni, who happily held it out to him. He laughed. "I was just kidding. That's yours. You keep it. Can you see the reindeer coming up?"

Sunni shook her head.

"Want to sit on my shoulders?" he asked. "You'll see all the floats from up there."

"Candy?" Her big blue eyes darted to the street where candy kept being tossed, then back to him. Leann doubted anything would keep her girl away from the promise of sweets.

"I'll get your candy, Sunni," Frank chimed in. "Leave it to Gramps."

"Thanks, Dad." Michael hoisted Sunni onto his shoulders. She gripped her little hands around his neck and giggled loudly.

Every now and then, someone would call out Michael's name and wave to him. Leann could see he was well liked, and it didn't surprise her in the slightest.

"Look, girls, there's Santa!" Patty, holding four-year-old Rachel's hand, pointed to the float approaching with Santa's sleigh and his reindeer. David and Kelli had skipped the parade. David was keeping the clinic open for a few hours this morning, while Kelli had stayed home with their two-year-old, Bobby, and the baby.

Leann couldn't believe how natural it felt to be with Michael and his family. They'd made her feel like she and Sunni belonged with them. Last night, they'd all watched Christmas movies after dinner. Then, one by one, his parents and Hannah had gone up to bed, leaving her alone with Michael. They'd talked until midnight. She'd told him about Luke and how their marriage ended almost as soon as it began, and he told her how close he'd gotten with his sister after she graduated from high school. He'd driven to the University of Montana to visit Hannah often, until he started working in Alberta.

As much as Leann enjoyed being with his family, she had to keep tamping down the rush of joy their company brought.

She didn't belong with them.

They were kind and generous, but this was a Christmas blip. Soon her wrist would be fine, she and Sunni would be living in their own apartment and Michael would be off researching somewhere else. She'd better not forget it.

"Rachel, I see Tootsie Rolls over there." Patty pointed in front of the snow pile next to them.

The tiny blonde was Kelli's spitting image, and with her sparkly pink stocking cap and matching coat, she looked like a little princess. "Thanks, Grammy. I'll get you one, too."

A marching band played "Santa Claus is Coming to Town," drowning out the laughter and conversations around them. The final float passed by, and Rachel, with Frank's help, scooped up stray candies, laughing all the while.

Michael set Sunni back down to get her candy from his dad. Rachel rushed over to hug Sunni, and Sunni hugged her right back. It was the sweetest thing—Leann's heart almost couldn't take it. Her daughter already had a friend.

"Who wants hot cocoa?" Patty asked.

"Cocoa!" Sunni whirled to face Michael, lifting her arms for him to carry her. Leann frowned. It was great that Sunni trusted him, but she'd grown attached in a miniscule amount of time. Did her sweet daughter crave having a daddy? How could Leann explain that Michael was just a friend? One who'd probably only be here for Christmas before moving on?

Maybe she was overthinking things.

He hoisted Sunni into his arms. "You don't like cocoa, do you?"

"Cocoa!"

"What do you say, Leann?" His eyes gleamed with happiness and…appreciation…for her.

Her stomach felt all fluttery.

"What's a little more sugar?" She shrugged, lifting her hands. A parade, candy and cocoa weren't going to hurt her little girl. But growing too attached to Michael could. And, if Leann were being honest with herself, it could hurt her, as well.

Sunni wasn't the only one enamored of Michael Carr.

Leann had better clamp down on her emotions soon, or it would be awfully lonely after Christmas.

Sunrise Bend was doing funny things to his heart.

Michael tossed the empty cup into the trash can as he kept a tight grip on Sunni, who had fallen asleep in his arms. The crowds were thinning out, and the nip in the air drove people off the streets and into the stores.

"Leann, I just got a text from my friend Joy," his mom said. "She and her husband, Leonard, own the candy shop down the block. The two-bedroom apartment above it will be available after Christmas. She said you can tour it now if you'd like."

The candy shop had been one of Michael's favorite hangouts as a kid. Whenever his parents would drive into town, he and David would beg to go in. They always left with a big bag of chocolates and sour gummies.

Sometimes he really missed his brother.

"Would you mind if I toured it?" Leann asked him. The worry in her eyes almost made him laugh. Did she think he had something better to do?

There was nothing else he'd rather do.

"Oh, go with her, Michael. Joy is leaving it unlocked." His mom waggled her finger at him. "You can inspect it and make sure there aren't any problems."

"You don't have to do that." Leann shook her head.

"I don't mind. Besides, I've got my orders." He hitched his chin. "Come on. It isn't far." He glanced at his parents. "We'll be home later."

"Want us to take Sunni?" Dad asked.

"Nah. The car seat is in my truck. We've got her."

"Okay, we'll see you kids later." With Rachel between them, his parents strolled away, holding the little girl's hands.

Leann scrambled to his side. "Really, Michael, you don't have to—"

"I want to." He paused in front of the jeweler's, looked down at her pretty face and wanted to do something more. Blame it on the festive air, but those full lips tempted him.

He hadn't been tempted to kiss a woman in a long time.

All he'd have to do is bend slightly...

Her eyelashes dipped, and she ducked her chin. "I feel bad. You've gone out of your way to help me, and I..."

What was she talking about? He tipped her chin up and stared into her eyes. "You think I'm doing you the favor, don't you?"

She nodded.

"You're wrong," he said quietly. "You've given me a reason to get reacquainted with my hometown. Before I met you, I'd planned on staying at the ranch the entire Christmas break."

"Why?" She sounded confused.

He gestured for them to keep walking. "I don't know. I guess it's awkward to be here. Back when Kelli and I were together, I'd gotten serious—considered proposing—before I found out she was dating my brother. Since then, Sunrise Bend has felt like their town. It sounds stupid saying it out loud..." He pointed ahead to an alley. "Let's cut through here. The door to the apartment should be in the back."

"It doesn't sound stupid. After Luke left me, I wouldn't drive in the neighborhood where his dental practice was because I was afraid of seeing him and Deb or them spotting me. I didn't want their pity."

Didn't want pity—that was it. He'd become an outsider in this town because he didn't want anyone's pity. However, since he'd been home, people had waved to him, greeted him in stores and generally acted like he'd never left.

Did anyone even remember he'd dated Kelli once upon a time?

When they reached the apartment door, he opened it, shifting Sunni to better hold her. He pointed to the staircase. "Ladies first."

He thought of his dad and the ranch chores. Of Hannah and his mom. Of the welcome many people in town had given him.

Maybe he'd been wrong to avoid Sunrise Bend.

Michael had been thinking about proposing to Kelli? Leann made her way up the stairs. Her life was already as topsy-turvy as a carnival ride. If his confession didn't pour buckets of snow all over her budding attraction for him, nothing would. It was a good reminder where her focus should be. On making a home here.

She emerged onto a landing and opened the door at the top. Michael followed her inside. A living room with distressed hardwood floors greeted her. It had a large picture window overlooking Main Street. The space was old but bright and clean. A kitchen to her right had space to put a small table and chairs. They found the bedrooms, one spacious, one tiny, and the bathroom—outdated but in good working order—and looked in all the closets. Then they returned to the living room.

"Is she getting too heavy?" Leann asked.

"Are you kidding?" He grinned. "I'm used to hauling firewood and supplies. She's a breeze to carry."

He always had the perfect thing to say. And that was a problem, because the more time she spent with him, the more she liked him. And not as a friend. He treated her like she was special, worth his attention, and she hadn't felt that way in a long time.

"I don't see any red flags," Michael said. "It's older, but in good condition."

"I like it." And she did. It would be fun to live above the candy store. "I can walk to work. And Sunni and I will be close to everything. We'll make good memories here."

He quickly stared down at the floor.

"What is it?" she asked. "Is it this place? Do you know something you're not telling me?"

"No, nothing like that. I...like it. A lot. I think you and Sunni would be very happy here."

"Then why did you grimace?"

"I didn't grimace."

"You did."

"You don't miss much, do you?" He raised his eyebrows. "I don't know. I haven't had a place to call my own in years, unless you count the apartment I shared with three guys during my final year of college."

A wave of sympathy hit her. "You want a home of your own, don't you?"

He didn't answer.

"Well, this place is available. Do you want it?" She closed the distance between them.

"No." His eyes darkened, shimmered. "Sunni will love it. It's perfect for you."

"You could move back, you know."

Shaking his head, he stepped away from her.

Disappointment burrowed in her gut. He wanted a home, but he didn't want one here. And why would he? Just because she wanted him to stay didn't mean he felt the same. He had things to do, wildlife to study.

The sooner Leann moved into an apartment, the sooner she could create some much-needed distance between her and Michael. She'd been foolish to spend so much time with him. He'd be leaving soon, and she'd be here. Trying not to think of him.

Chapter Seven

Michael wanted this. All of it.

Sunday evening, children dressed as shepherds, angels and sheep recited verses from the second chapter of Luke at the front of the church. A scaled-down replica of a stable had been set up, and two teens were playing the parts of Mary and Joseph. One little shepherd was waving his staff like a lightsaber, and two of the sheep were giggling.

He wanted to sit in the same row as his parents watching the nativity play each year. He wanted a wife and family to celebrate the holidays with. He longed to see his own children dressed as sheep and shepherds and angels up front.

He wanted to build a real life. A full one. He might even want it right here in Sunrise Bend.

And the thought terrified him and filled him with hope at the same time.

Leann sat next to him, her delicate perfume teasing his senses. When the kids finished their recitation, soft harp music drifted from the loudspeakers. His niece, Rachel, a sheep, lifted her hand high in the air to wave to them. Sunni jumped up on the pew to wave back to her. Leann tried to lower Sunni's arm, but the child continued to wave, yelling, "Raycho," and, red-faced, Leann shushed her.

David and Kelli were seated on the other side of his parents. Earlier when they'd arrived, he'd nodded and said a silent prayer of thanks that he hadn't had to speak to either of them. Their toddler son, Bobby, sat on Mom's lap and pretended to make a toy car fly through the air. Whispers had traveled to Michael that his brother and Kelli had left the baby at home with a babysitter. Like he cared.

Shame skittered over his skin. This was his family. He should care.

It was sad that he felt closer to Sunni than to his own niece and nephews. He barely knew David's children. They seemed like cute, polite kids. With a lot of energy. But the same could be said about most children.

Did he really want to go through the rest of his life estranged from his brother? Not knowing his kin?

The children sang a short song, and the pastor read from the Bible before launching into a sermonette about trust. How Joseph had to trust God by marrying Mary, who was pregnant. How Mary had to trust God by traveling to Bethlehem at the end of her pregnancy.

"The book of Proverbs tells us to 'Trust in the Lord with all thine heart; and lean not unto thine own understanding. In all thy ways acknowledge Him, and He shall direct thy paths.' This Christmas season, I ask you to look inward. Are you acknowledging Him? Do you trust Him? Really trust Him? Even when things are going wrong? God loves you. You can count on Him to direct your path. You'll never regret it. Amen."

The choir began singing "Silent Night," leaving Michael to ponder the pastor's words. He'd been on his current career path for a long time. Had God directed him there? Probably. Getting out of town and staying out had seemed like the only way forward after finding out about his brother's betrayal. And in the ensuing years, he hadn't considered other options.

Michael glanced at Leann as she sang the hymn. She looked peaceful. Content.

He'd love to have someone like her by his side.

A flash of blond hair at the end of the row caught his eye. Kelli stood and walked to the back of the church. Seeing her no longer affected him. Sure, she was pretty, but her looks didn't do anything for him like they had back when they'd dated.

But…if he'd been wrong about Kelli, who was to say he wasn't wrong about Leann, too?

Leann was more grounded than Kelli had been. She was older, more mature. Had a child to raise. But it didn't change the fact that he barely knew her. She seemed interested in him, but maybe it was circumstantial. Would she still look at him like he was her personal hero after her car was fixed and she moved into an apartment?

He'd be gone soon, anyhow.

What if he stayed?

His heart began to thump.

Sunni yawned and held her arms up to him. He lifted her onto his lap, and she settled in, resting her dark curls against his chest.

After Christmas, there wouldn't be parades and festivities. January brought bitter cold weather and not much else. The question was—did he want to spend it in Alaska or here?

And if he chose Sunrise Bend, would Leann be interested in getting to know him better?

He wished he knew the answer.

"He's so precious." Leann couldn't get over how exquisite little Owen was. Kelli had been bouncing him to get him to stop crying when Leann asked if she could hold him. Looking desperate, Kelli had thrust the baby to her, but Leann's wrist was still tender, so she'd sat on the couch and waited for Kelli to set him in her arms.

He'd cried and cried for ten minutes, but keeping him on her lap, Leann had rolled him onto his tummy and patted his back until his cries dwindled to a whimper. Then she'd turned him over once more and held him gently, not putting pressure on her wrist, until he'd fallen asleep.

"I haven't held a baby in forever. Sunni is growing up too fast." Leann traced his tiny eyebrows with her index finger, reveling in his soft baby skin. "I could just eat him up. He's darling."

"You know what's darling?" Kelli set a tray of cheese and crackers on the coffee table in front of several women from church. "Listen. Do you hear that? He's not crying."

The women laughed, and Leann agreed. No crying was a good thing.

The men stood in a group in the adjoining den where a football game played on the television. Giggles and excited chatter could be heard from the corner where half a dozen small kids played with toys. With Bumbles in her lap, Sunni sat cross-legged next to Rachel. The girls looked as happy as could be.

As the women discussed holiday plans, Leann took it all in. The big house. The friends. The kids. The fire in the fireplace. Frank tugging Patty under the mistletoe and kissing her on the cheek. Patty blushing and waving at him. "Oh, Frank, stop!" Frank pulling her closer and giving her a chaste kiss on the lips. "Frank!" He grinned, winking at her before heading back into the den with the guys.

Leann wanted this.

All of it.

A house, a fireplace, friends and—she glanced at Michael, who was standing in the den off to the side staring at his phone—a husband. A man who would stick around and love her. Marry her. Give her another baby.

She sighed and looked down tenderly at Owen once more.

Michael would probably leave after the holidays, so there was no point weaving a fantasy with him as the husband of her dreams.

His discomfort at being here was obvious. He'd barely said two words. She peeked his way again, but he wasn't in the den. Where had he gone? Was the party too much for him? Did being here remind him of how much he missed Kelli?

A lump formed in her throat, and she forced herself to concentrate on the baby. If she'd been smarter like Luke's new wife or vivacious like Kelli, maybe she'd have a husband, a house, a room full of friends.

Leann had never been at the same level as women like them.

"I didn't have a chance to tell you my news earlier." Hannah smooshed in next to her on the couch.

"What is it? What's going on?" Leann willed her emotions to settle. No pity parties. Not tonight.

"One of the second-grade teachers is going on maternity leave in early February, and Sunrise Bend Elementary hired me to be her long-term substitute. Isn't it great?"

"It's wonderful! Congratulations, Hannah." She tried to reach over to give her a hug, but she didn't want to disturb the baby, so she patted her arm instead.

"Let me take this little butterball." Patty swept Owen into her arms, cradling him. "Look at those cheeks."

"I know," Leann said. "He's just the cutest."

After Patty took Owen, Hannah crossed one leg over the other. "Everyone told me I'd probably have to move far away to get a teaching job, but I've always wanted to teach here. It's home."

"I understand, and I think getting experience through substituting is a smart move. Who knows? Maybe someone will retire, and the school will snatch you up."

"I hope you're right. I wish Michael would stick around, too. I miss him. It's been great having him home for more than forty-eight hours."

Leann didn't know what to say, so she nodded in agreement.

"Now I need to find myself a boyfriend." Hannah pretended to dust off her shoulders. "When you settle in at the store, you'll have to let me know if you hear of any single hotties in town."

Leann laughed. "I'll make it my mission. Any preferences?"

"Well, he needs to be comfortable on horseback. A hard worker. And cute. Very cute."

"No problem. I'll get right on it." She glanced around the living room. "Could you direct me to the powder room?"

"Sure." Hannah pointed toward the kitchen. "Pass the kitchen and take a right down the hall. It's across from David's study."

"Thanks."

Leann stood and checked on Sunni before following Hannah's directions. The fact that Hannah would be sticking around Sunrise Bend was a good thing. She liked Michael's energetic sister. She hoped to get to know her better.

And, like Hannah, she wished Michael would stick around town, too.

As Leann approached the powder-room door, she heard male voices nearby.

"You're not over Kelli, are you?" She recognized David's voice. Her heartbeat began to pound. She expected

Michael to reply, but when he didn't, she darted into the powder room and locked the door.

Maybe it would be better if Michael didn't stay after the holidays. She was already halfway in love with him, and if he was still pining for Kelli, Leann had no chance with him. None at all.

Chapter Eight

"Is that what you think?" Michael asked quietly. David had dragged him into the study a few minutes ago, and Michael hadn't put up a fight. This evening had given him clarity. He was tired of hanging on to resentment and bitterness over the past. He was ready to let it go.

"I don't know." David padded to the window then turned back to him. "You won't talk to me."

"You haven't exactly tried."

"I'm sorry, Michael. I am." David sighed. "When you introduced me to Kelli right before you left for that research job, I was fully prepared to do as you asked and look out for her."

Michael ground his teeth together. As much as he wanted to interject with a snide comment, he held his tongue.

"I didn't mean to fall in love. Every time I told myself to put the brakes on my feelings, I'd see her smile and forget everything."

What kind of apology was this? Michael balled his hands into fists.

"But it was wrong. I was wrong. I knew it then, and I know it now. I'm sorry. I want my brother back. I miss you. I can't tell you how much I've missed you. Can you ever forgive me?"

All the tension building in Michael's chest began to subside. Over the years, he'd pictured himself screaming at David for betraying him, but the apology changed things. Michael found he didn't care all that much anymore. Seeing Kelli at church and here at their house did nothing for him. Dad was right. Kelli wasn't the woman for him.

Michael only had eyes for Leann.

"I needed to hear it, David." Michael stood tall. "I forgive you."

"Just like that?" David frowned.

"Yeah. I've been over Kelli for a long time. What I wasn't over was what you did. I've missed you, too."

"I should have apologized a long time ago. I'm sorry." He looked thoughtful. "Have you been serious with anyone? Like the research partner you always team up with?"

"Jan?" Michael laughed. "Nope. We're colleagues. Nothing more."

"Anyone else?"

"No."

"Why not?"

"Because I haven't had feelings for anyone since Kelli, okay?" The words were true…well, they had been up until a few days ago when he'd met Leann.

An awkward silence grew between them.

"What's next for you?" David asked. "This is the longest you've been home in years."

"I'm not sure. Jan has a research gig lined up in Alaska. She wants me to join her."

"I'm surprised you haven't jumped at the chance."

Michael was, too. But something felt different this year. He'd known he needed to be here with his family. "I guess I need a little time to figure out my next step."

"What are the options?" David moved closer to him.

"Alaska, obviously." He couldn't quite believe he and David were having a normal conversation. Like nothing had ever happened. But it *had* happened…

Let it go.

"And I get calls every other month about working as a game warden for the state of Wyoming." Michael didn't want the job. Lately, a different future enticed.

"You'd be great at it," David said. "Where would you live?"

"I don't know. Haven't crossed that bridge. Working the cattle this past week with Dad's been nice. Real nice."

"Are you saying…?" David's face lit up.

"I'm considering it."

"If you took over the ranch…man, that would be great! I'd love to have you back."

Strange how full his heart suddenly felt after being shriveled into a tight knot for so long.

"Like I said, I've got some thinking to do. I haven't talked to Dad yet, either, so keep a lid on it."

"Well, keep thinking. I'm here if you want to talk. Just imagine, if you moved back, we could watch football together, take a ski trip, go hunting…" David pulled him into a hug. "Thanks for showing me grace, Michael. I love you."

His throat tightened. "I love you, too."

Well, wonders never ceased. He had his brother back.

What else would this Christmas have in store for him?

Her heart was on the verge of crumbling. It wasn't Michael's fault she liked him so much. Leann washed her hands and checked her appearance in the mirror. This room, like the rest of the house, was luxurious and welcoming. The thick, fluffy towel was a far cry from her own threadbare ones packed into boxes in a storage facility back home.

It was time to mentally move on.

Tomorrow she was calling the apartment complex Michael had suggested, but she had a feeling she'd be putting a deposit down on the apartment above the candy shop instead. The location was perfect, and the size was just right for her and Sunni. After Leann banked a couple paychecks, she'd buy a few things for their place. New hand towels had jumped to the top of her list.

Making a home, a nice life, had been her objective all along. Not falling for the handsome man who was still carrying a torch for her boss.

She checked the mirror once more before striding out to the hall and back to the living room. She would just have to keep a smile plastered on her face and get through this party as best as she could.

Sitting on the couch once more, she couldn't help but stare at Kelli, who tilted her head back to laugh at something one of the women said.

Kelli with her shiny wavy blond hair. Wearing a tasteful cream satin blouse nipped at the waist with tiny bows at the sleeves. She looked put-together, stunning, sophisticated. Her eyes sparkled. She was the epitome of a gracious hostess—charming, self-deprecating. No wonder Michael had been in love with her. Still might care for her. What guy wouldn't?

Sunni toddled over to Leann and plopped Bumbles on the couch next to her. Yawning, she tried to climb onto Leann's lap but couldn't quite get there. Leann tugged with her good hand and helped her up. Wrapping her arms around her sweet daughter, she kissed her curls.

"You tired, sweetie?"

"Bubba go night night." Sunni snuggled the rabbit and sank into Leann's arms.

"He's pretty tuckered out, isn't he?" She rested her temple against Sunni's head and inhaled the baby shampoo she'd used to wash her hair. Sunni and Bumbles weren't the only ones who were tired. Weariness sank into Leann's bones, and the conversations around her seemed to fade into the background.

Noticing movement, she glanced over and caught Michael staring at her. The gleam in his eye was appreciative.

Her cheeks grew warm. The way he was looking at her...

Could she be wrong about him still pining for Kelli?

She averted her gaze. The long pause after David had asked him point-blank if he was over Kelli had been telling. And even if he was over her, it didn't change anything. He loved his job, and that meant living in the wilderness for long lengths of time. Leann suppressed a sigh. The way his face had brightened when he'd told her about the things he did to research fish had said it all. He had a passion— a gift—for his work.

Which meant after Christmas, he'd be moving on.

And she'd be moving on, too. Here. With Sunni. All she had to do was think of the day Luke had told her he was moving to Costa Rica to remind herself of the promise she'd made. The only guy she'd consider dating was one who would be around for her and her precious girl.

Too bad the one man she wanted was Michael. All of the kindness he'd shown her over the previous days piled up like precious gifts in her heart. It wasn't his fault she'd grown feelings for him. Just because she was disappointed didn't mean she couldn't show him how much she appreciated everything he'd done for her.

"Hannah?" Leann leaned over to catch her attention.

"What?"

"Are you busy this week?"

"I'm filling in at the clinic tomorrow." Hannah screwed up her lips and looked at the ceiling. "I'm off Tuesday, why?"

"I was wondering if you would drive me into town."

"Me?" She looked confused. "I thought Michael would—"

"He's been more than generous with his time. I'd like to get him something to repay his kindness."

"Oh, I see." Understanding dawned on Hannah's face. "Sure, Leann, I'll take you into town for a little something." She gave her an exaggerated stare.

Leann chuckled. Hannah had a way of saying things that cracked her up.

"Thanks." Hopefully, she'd find him a meaningful gift. But even if she purchased a fabulous present, it wouldn't suffice. Because all she really wanted to give him was her heart.

Chapter Nine

After another morning of breaking ice on the creek, dropping a line of feed in the pasture, checking cattle and cleaning out horse stalls with his dad, Michael was 99 percent sure he knew what he wanted. And it wasn't Alaska.

"I've been thinking about what you said the other day." Michael followed his father into the ranch office located inside the stables Tuesday afternoon. He and Leann had spent yesterday afternoon playing with Sunni, drinking hot cocoa and petting all the cats and dogs in the barns. Sunni had grown smitten with Molasses, an old basset hound. Molasses hadn't minded when Sunni plopped down next to her and delicately petted her ears for what felt like forever.

"About what?" Dad took a seat in a beat-up chair and gestured for Michael to join him on a nearby stool.

"The ranch's future."

"Oh, yeah?" Dad perked up. "Let's hear what you have to say."

"I don't want you to retire." He took off his gloves and set them on the desk, then cupped his cold hands and blew on them.

"It's not up to you, son."

"I know," Michael said. "But I'm asking you to stay on for another year or two."

"Why?"

"Because I think it's time I settled down. And this ranch is in my blood. I love it—have always loved it. I want to work with you, Dad. And when you're ready to retire, I want to be the one to keep it going."

With tears in his eyes, Dad stood. "I never thought I'd hear those words. You mean it? You want to work with this old geezer?"

"Old? You're just coming into your prime." Michael laughed. "And, yes, I mean it."

"Thank you." His dad wrapped him into a bear hug for what seemed like forever. "We'll work out the details to be fair to David and Hannah."

"Of course."

"Have you said anything to your mother, yet?" Dad reclaimed his seat, leaning back with his hands over his stomach.

"No. I wanted to talk to you first."

"She is going to bawl her eyes out, Michael. She's going to be so happy. Hey, why don't you do me a favor. Wait until Christmas Eve or Christmas Day to tell her. You know how hard it is to find your mother the perfect gift. Nothing will make her happier than to know you're coming home for good *and* taking over the ranch."

"I can do that." He hadn't thought about how his mom would react. His dad was right—she'd be pleased.

"What about the research, though?" Dad's expression grew serious. "You know we're proud of you. If you have unfinished business with it…well, we know how much you love your job."

"I do love it. I did, at least. I want other things now."

Dad nodded.

"Besides, we have enough property." Michael thought of the thousands of acres on Carr Ranch. "I can always track wildlife here. Then I won't get rusty. There are plenty of rivers nearby to study fish, too. I'm not worried about it."

"I never thought of that." Dad rubbed his chin. "What happens next? Are you staying here for good? Or do you have loose ends to wrap up with your last gig?"

"My supplies are in storage. I need to tell Jan I won't be coming to Alaska. Beyond that, I'm all set. Looks like I'm here to stay."

Dad grinned. "Let's talk about living arrangements. Obviously, you can stay in the house with us, but if you want to move into the lodge, we can get it cleaned up."

The lodge was a three-bedroom log home situated on the other side of the ranch with a view of the river and mountains. His grandparents had lived in it when he was a kid.

"I'd like living there." Michael couldn't think of a better place to come home to each night.

"It would be a nice place to raise a family."

"One thing at a time, Dad." He instantly pictured Leann and Sunni with him at the lodge. Decorating a tree for Christmas. Rocking on the front porch in the summer. Yes, the lodge would be a great place to raise a family.

"Don't wait too long. Leann is a fine woman. Once the cowboys 'round here get wind of her, you might have some competition."

He hadn't thought of that. What chance would he have with her when the other guys started falling all over themselves to woo her? And why was he using the term *woo*, anyhow? He sounded like an old grandpa.

Maybe he wasn't giving himself—or Leann—enough

credit. Just because Kelli had dropped him in a hot second when another guy came along didn't mean Leann would, too.

This town got cuter and cuter with each passing day. Sunshine glinted off the outdoor decorations on Main Street. Leann strolled next to Hannah on their way to the bait-and-tackle shop. Sunni had stayed at the ranch with Patty, who insisted they have a tea-and-cookie party. Sunni, naturally, had loved the idea.

"You didn't like it, did you?" Hannah asked. They'd just toured an empty two-bedroom apartment in a complex outside of town.

"I liked it but not as much as the apartment above the candy shop." Leann opened the door marked Watkins Outfitters and waited for Hannah to enter before going inside. "When we're through in here, I'd like to stop in the candy store to put a deposit down."

"Fine with me. I've got a craving for a slice of Joy's peanut butter fudge." Hannah lingered near a small shelf of books. "If I had a full-time job, I would probably rent a one-bedroom apartment in the complex you looked at today."

"I wouldn't blame you." Leann stopped, unsure of what she was looking for. She took in the shelves of lures, nets and poles. "I have no idea what to get Michael."

"I do." Hannah grinned. "Follow me."

Leann obeyed.

"Hey, Randy. Did you get the new book in?"

An attractive man in his midtwenties wiped his hands on a paper towel and came out from behind the counter. "Which one? *Neuroscience of Bears*?"

Hannah gave him a long stare full of scorn. "Bears? Really? You know I meant the fish one."

"Yeah, I got it." His teeth gleamed under a cocky grin. "It's in the back. Give me a minute."

"What about him?" Leann nudged Hannah as Randy ambled to the back.

"What about him?" She looked confused.

"He's cute. You mentioned wanting a boyfriend..."

"Randy?" Her whisper carried. "Are you out of your mind? Eww."

"Sorry. I didn't realize he was so horrifying to you."

"He's not..." Hannah grimaced. "I wouldn't say horrifying, but he's more like my brother. I can't mentally go there."

"With those brown eyes, you might want to mentally go there." Leann blinked innocently.

Hannah chewed the corner of her lip and tried to peek around the bend where Randy had disappeared. "Nope. Can't do it."

"Okay, looks like I'm still on find-you-a-boyfriend duty."

"And don't forget my criteria." Hannah waved a finger in front of her. "Anyway, I was going to give this book to Michael for Christmas, but I found him a cool fishing net instead. Now you can give the book to him."

"Oh, I feel bad. I don't want to take your gift."

"You didn't. Like I said, I got him the net." Her laugh tinkled merrily. "He'll love it."

"Okay, but if you change your mind and want to give it to him yourself, just let me know." Leann drifted to the other side of the store, where assorted fishing and hunting gifts had been displayed. A picture frame with Gone Fishing on it caught her eye. A small artificial tree was decorated with beautiful painted-glass ornaments shaped like salmon, trout, bass and others she didn't recognize. Best of all, they were on sale.

They were perfect. She picked up a shopping basket and selected half a dozen ornaments. Michael was going to love them. He'd told her he didn't have a home, and she doubted he owned Christmas ornaments or the other things that naturally came with living in his own place. Even if he continued traveling for research, at some point he'd settle down. This would give him a start on his Christmas decorations. And when he unpacked them, maybe he'd think of her…and remember this time together.

All of the little moments with Michael came to mind. His blue eyes the night he'd found her. The way he helped with Sunni and treated them both so sweetly. The coffees, the parade, decorating cookies and sitting next to him at the nativity play on Sunday.

He was everything she wanted in a man.

Her vision blurred. She set the basket down.

She was way past crush territory.

"Is something wrong? You look green all of a sudden." Hannah approached her.

"I'm fine." She attempted to smile. She wasn't, though. She wasn't fine at all. "I'll take the book, and I'm getting these, too."

"Are you sure you're okay? The flu has been going around."

Leann wished it was a mere case of the flu. Seven to ten days and she'd be back to normal. Unfortunately, there wasn't a cure for what she had…or for the broken heart sure to be left in its wake.

Chapter Ten

Leann followed Hannah into the ranch's kitchen an hour later. She'd put a deposit down on the apartment over the candy shop, and she'd be able to move in next Saturday, two days after Christmas. The timing was perfect. Her wrist should be much better by then. Life in Sunrise Bend was coming together.

Being with Hannah had taken Leann's mind off the inconvenient fact she was pretty sure she'd lost her heart to Michael, which must be a world record since she'd known him just shy of a week. To distract herself, all the way home she'd teased Hannah about Randy, and Hannah had come up with increasingly outrageous reasons why they would never work as a couple.

"Knock, knock." Kelli walked in the front door. "Oh, good, Leann, you're here. I needed to speak with you."

What was Kelli doing here? And why did she want to see her? Leann tried to think of a good reason, and all she could come up with was maybe Kelli wanted her to start work sooner than their agreed-upon date. She set her shopping bags near the staircase.

"Can I talk to you in private?" Kelli hitched her head toward the living room, where the decorated tree stood tall in front of the picture window. Sunlight streamed in, making the space bright.

"Sure."

"Want me to take your packages upstairs, Leann?" Hannah asked, pausing near the staircase.

"Yes, please."

Kelli led the way to the couch and checked that Hannah was upstairs before speaking.

"Look, Leann, there's no easy way to say this…" Kelli wouldn't look her in the eye. Was this about Michael? Had Kelli figured out she had feelings for him and was trying to warn her away? Acid brewed in her stomach.

"What's going on?" Leann asked.

"While I love my kids and want to spend more time with them, I don't think it's the right time for me to pull back from The Sassy Lasso. There's too much inventory to keep track of, and I don't think you're ready for it. I'm staying on as manager."

This couldn't be happening. The air whooshed out of her lungs. The job she'd been so excited about—the one she'd moved here for—was no longer hers?

"I don't understand—"

"I don't expect you to." Kelli raised her palm. "I feel really bad, but I have too much at stake."

"But you didn't even give me a chance. Could we at least do a trial run? If you don't think I can handle the job after two weeks, say the word." There had to be a way to salvage this.

"My mind is made up." Kelli stood abruptly and smoothed her tight red sweater over her jeans. "I'm sorry, Leann. Truly."

Truly? Somehow Leann didn't believe it. What could she do to change Kelli's mind?

The future she'd been counting on was being snatched

from her grasp. Without a job, a new life in Sunrise Bend wouldn't make sense. She stood, too, holding on to the thinnest thread of hope.

"Let's just try—"

"I don't want there to be hard feelings." Kelli turned to leave, jumping back. "Oh, Michael. I didn't see you there."

Leann met his eyes and almost shrank back at the anger blazing in them.

Kelli, head high, scurried to the foyer. The soft thud of the door assured Leann she'd left.

Only then did her knees buckle, landing her back on the couch. She cradled her forehead in her hands, willing herself not to panic. She sensed Michael's presence next to her. Flinched when he took a seat and put his arm around her shoulders.

She couldn't look at him. This was humiliation to the nth degree.

"I'm sorry," he said.

She straightened, keeping her focus on the Christmas tree.

"Will you look at me?" he asked gently.

She shook her head. If she looked at him, she'd start bawling.

"I should have warned you about her. She doesn't think about how her decisions affect others."

Inhaling deeply, she tried to swallow the lump in her throat. "I should have known this was too good to be true. I just…wanted it so badly. It's not the first time I trusted the wrong person. I feel so stupid."

"Hey, it's not your fault."

She faced him then. "It doesn't matter whose fault it is. Doesn't change reality. I just put a deposit down on the apartment above the candy store. And now I have no job. What a disaster."

"Get a different job."

"Right. I'm sure there are oodles of positions for me here. Even if there were, I can't imagine running into Kelli all the time now that…" She shook her head. "What am I going to do? I needed this, Michael. I needed it. I had it all mapped out. I was going to make a new life here, a good life for Sunni. How am I going to do that now? Maybe I can get my deposit back."

"It's going to work out."

"It's not." The last thread of her patience snapped. "It's not working out. Nothing in my life ever does."

"We'll think of something."

"There's no we. You're leaving after Christmas. I… I'll…" She couldn't think straight. All her dreams and hopes were disappearing before her very eyes.

"What if I didn't leave?"

She met his eyes then. Intense, vulnerable, yearning.

"Why would you stay? Unless…you're not over Kelli, are you?"

"I'm over Kelli." How could Leann say that? Wasn't she picking up on his cues? Hadn't she seen how he'd been looking at her for days? Michael flexed his hands. "I've been over her for a long time."

"Then why is there so much tension between you and her and David? If you were over her, you wouldn't avoid them."

"Look, David and I talked at his house the other night. We're all right. We worked things out."

"Really?" Her big blue eyes glistened with unshed tears. He wanted to crush her to him and take away her pain. And he wanted to throttle Kelli for being so cruel.

"Yes."

"I'm glad." She attempted to smile but her face fell.

"I'm not going to Alaska."

Something flickered in her eyes, putting him on alert.

"Are you sure that's what's best for you?" She rubbed her forearm. "You love your job. Your entire face lights up when you talk about trout populations and river samples."

"So?" Michael clenched his jaw. He really sounded as boring as he thought when she put it like that.

"You can't give up on your passion." She tilted her chin up. "And your passion is helping restore fish populations. You wouldn't be doing that here, would you?"

"No, I wouldn't."

"Then why would you stay?"

How could he explain his feelings? He tried on half a dozen words but none of them came out of his mouth.

"Your job is important."

His heart fell. He wasn't dumb. She was letting him down easy in her kind way.

"Point taken." He rose quickly. "You don't have to say another word."

She stood, too. "I wasn't trying to make a point, Michael."

"It's fine. Sorry I made you feel uncomfortable."

"You didn't. I like you, Michael." She shook her head, staring off to the side. "But you shouldn't give up a career you love. Maybe it's best we put the brakes on whatever we're feeling. I need a man who will stick around, and you'll leave again. Research is in your blood. Sunni's my number one priority, and I'm—"

"Got it." He turned to leave. He couldn't expect her to have feelings for him the way he had for her—not in a matter of days. "I…I have to go."

He tried to keep his composure until he got to the mudroom. Then he threw on his coat and boots and jogged straight to his truck.

His heart was expanding and contracting to the point he thought something might be seriously wrong with it.

Then it hit him.

Something *was* seriously wrong with it.

He'd fallen in love.

And she'd rejected him.

Or maybe he'd misread the situation from the beginning.

Either way, she wasn't interested. And, once more, he was stuck with a broken heart.

Chapter Eleven

"Thanks for watching her for me." Leann found Sunni and Patty upstairs in Hannah's room a few minutes later. The three of them were singing Christmas songs and playing with Bumbles. Leann had barely composed herself before coming to find them.

"Mama!" Sunni ran to her.

"Were you a good girl?"

Her daughter nodded happily.

"She's always good. We just love having her around." Patty's tone was so tender, it brought a lump to Leann's throat.

"Thank you. We're going to rest a bit. Tell Miss Patty thank you."

"Fank you, Gwammy." Sunni hugged Patty and toddled back to Leann. So sweet. As if Leann's heart could take any more...

She gave Hannah and Patty what she hoped would pass for a smile and left the room. Hannah hurried out to the hall. "Leann, is everything all right?"

"Not really." She should tell Hannah everything was fine, but she didn't have it in her. "I got some bad news."

"Is there anything we can do to help?"

"You and your family have helped me more than you know. I appreciate how you took us in. You've gone above anything I could have dreamed." Leann hugged Hannah, who stood there with a worried look on her face. Then, holding Sunni's hand, she continued down the hall to their room.

Inside, she boosted Sunni onto the bed, then spread out on top of the comforter as Sunni snuggled into her side.

"I wuv you, Mama."

"I love you, too, Sunni." Mindlessly, she stroked her daughter's soft curls and let her thoughts have free reign.

She had the feeling she'd hurt Michael just now. But how? What had she said that was so bad? She'd been trying to tell him she cared about him, and because she cared about him, she didn't want him to give up on a career he found rewarding. But the words must have come out all wrong.

Why had Michael been so abrupt when she'd told him his job was important? *Got it... Point taken.* She hadn't been trying to make a point, and he acted like she was blowing him off.

Leann squeezed her eyes shut. Maybe she was blowing him off. She didn't believe he'd stay in Sunrise Bend. Why would he? Regardless, she'd ruined it. All of it. The Sassy Lasso. The guy. The new life in the cute new town.

Glancing down at Sunni, she felt a yawning sense of failure.

God, what do I do now? I thought I had it all figured out. I was so sure this was the right move.

The days after Luke announced he'd fallen in love with Deb and moved out whizzed back to her mind. She'd been dumbfounded. Blindsided. She'd become unimportant and insignificant in a split second.

Kelli's words had produced the same effect.

Why in the world had Kelli decided Leann wasn't right for the job?

Was it because of Michael? Or was Kelli some kind of control freak?

Oh, what did it matter? The result was the same.

And just like she'd been forced to do after Luke left, Leann was going to have to figure out how to pick up the pieces and move on.

Her conscience prodded, poked, and she tried to ignore it. Michael had said he was staying, that he wasn't going to Alaska. Why didn't she believe him?

Because he so obviously loved what he did for a living.

But…why else would he stay?

Not because of Kelli. That was obvious now.

The moment in the apartment over the candy shop hit her again. He missed having a home. Wanted a place of his own.

She looked at Sunni, who was on the verge of sleep. Even if Michael stayed, it might not be long term. He'd miss researching fish. He'd be off again. Living like a nomad.

And if she explored a relationship with him, she'd have to watch him pack up and leave. It would break her heart. Knowing no matter what she did or said, he loved something else more than her. Only this time Sunni would be old enough to understand what was going on, and her little girl would truly know what it meant to lose an important man in her life.

Leann's heart was being crushed on all sides, but for her daughter's sake, she couldn't fall apart.

She'd do whatever it took to give Sunni a good, happy life.

She just needed to figure out how.

* * *

Michael shivered as he hiked on the public nature trail outside town. The sky was growing dark, but he had no desire to head back home. Although he'd been trying to pay attention to the various animal markings—coyotes had left scat at a crossroads on the trail and elk had been this way recently—nothing could divert his thoughts from Leann.

Was he rushing things? So desperate for love and a family that he'd projected his feelings onto Leann?

He thought back on the week they'd spent together. She was easy to talk to, hardworking, a loving mother. She had integrity. And whenever he was around her, he felt like he belonged right there by her side.

He'd handled things badly this afternoon. Walking in on Kelli destroying Leann's dreams had made him want to call down thunder and lightning on his ex. It was bad enough she'd hurt him, but needlessly hurting Leann? Unforgivable.

Kelli didn't need to manage the store. She had it all—a successful doctor for a spouse, a thriving business, three cute kids and a mini mansion. Yet, it hadn't been enough. So unwilling to share anything, she'd snatched Leann's future from her. He wanted to wring Kelli's neck.

He kicked at a clump of brush. Maybe he wasn't being fair. He didn't know Kelli anymore. She'd been ambitious back when they'd dated. She'd done well for herself, and he'd give her her due there. She probably had her own reasons for wanting to continue managing the store.

One thing this week had given him was clarity.

He could see Kelli was all wrong for him. And all right for David.

Michael liked quiet nights and simple pleasures. Kelli and David liked friends and social gatherings and...

He didn't really know. He didn't know them anymore.

But he did know how he felt about Leann. He hadn't put up much of a fight back there. So convinced she was blowing him off, he'd shut down and left.

He shoved his hands into his pockets and picked up the pace toward where he'd parked his truck.

He hadn't told her about missing the ranch and the work that went with it. Hadn't explained that Sunrise Bend was a part of him, and he missed it more than he'd realized. He hadn't told her how he felt about her. And he hadn't given her much of a chance to tell him how she felt about him, either.

How *did* she feel about him?

Well, considering she'd just heard terrible news, he shouldn't have expected her to fall into his arms declaring her undying affections.

She *had* told him she liked him. But she'd been concerned about his feelings for Kelli and for his job and…

He stopped in his tracks.

She did care about him. Enough to want him to be happy.

Maybe she'd needed reassurance. A declaration. Maybe she'd been feeling him out to see where his head was at. And he, stupidly, had taken it as a rejection.

Turning his face up to the sky, he let out a growl. Why didn't he understand these things? He was an idiot when it came to women.

Slowly, he pressed forward. What Leann had told him about her ex-husband began to fit into his mind better. How he'd left her for another woman who worked closely with him, and then he'd left the country, not caring that he wouldn't have a relationship with his daughter.

Didn't the guy have a clue how blessed he was to be able to call Sunni his own? Michael would give about anything for the same right. The precious toddler had stolen his heart.

And her mother had, too.

Leann had told him she needed a man who would stick around. And what had Michael done? He'd walked out the door.

God, I don't know what to do. Tomorrow is Christmas Eve. Am I being selfish for wanting Leann and Sunni in my life? Maybe I'm not what she needs. Help me get this right. Will You do like the pastor said and make my path straight?

His truck came into view. One thing was for sure—he didn't want to be another source of pain in Leann's life. She'd been through too much already.

Chapter Twelve

Leann shot up in the bed. The clock said 7:45 a.m. Sunni still slept beside her with Bumbles tucked in her arms. Her rosy cheeks made Leann want to stare at her for hours. Instead, she kissed her finger and touched Sunni's forehead with it.

It was Christmas Eve, and she didn't know how to salvage her plans. She needed to clear the air with Michael… if only she knew how. All night her mind had kept tromping around old hurts and new questions. She squeezed her eyes shut. *God, I'm scared. I'm scared I'm not enough for him. What if I take a chance and he decides I'm not good enough like Luke did, like Kelli just did?*

Maybe a shower would give her fresh insight.

She grabbed a towel and locked the bathroom door. She wasn't giving Michael the credit he deserved. Luke had made promises without backing them up. Michael was the exact opposite. His actions spoke for him. He would never let her down the way her ex-husband had. Michael had shown her he was a man of his word.

As she stared at her reflection in the mirror, her fears melted away. Instead of seeing blue eyes and messy hair, she saw a woman who spent too much time believing the worst about herself.

God, I have to give myself more credit, too, don't I? I have to believe I'm enough for him because I know I'm enough for You. Help me figure out how to tell him.

Fifteen minutes later, freshly showered and dressed, she bumped into Hannah in the hall. "Oh, I'm sorry. I didn't see you there."

"I heard what Kelli did." Hannah was shaking her head. "I can't believe she went back on her job offer. I am *this* close to telling her off."

Leann swallowed the lump in her throat. Funny, how good it felt to have someone on her side. "Oh, no. Please don't."

"She's been going on and on for months about wanting to spend more time with the kids, then she hires you and all of a sudden she *needs* to be at the store? I get the store is a lot quieter than being at home with Owen howling all day, but…"

Leann blinked, not hearing the rest of Hannah's words.

That was it! Kelli wasn't worried about the store failing, nor did she believe Leann was incompetent. She was scared. Scared of taking care of those kids all day by herself. With Owen's colic, who could blame her?

God, I'm right, aren't I?

An idea blossomed, and as it grew, Leann knew she was going to fight for it—all of it. The job she'd longed for. And the man of her dreams.

Her new life in Sunrise Bend was no longer cancelled.

"Thank you!" Leann threw her arms around Hannah. "I have another huge favor to ask of you, and I've already used up too many to count."

"What are you talking about?" Hannah's forehead scrunched.

"I need to talk to Kelli. Can you keep an eye on Sunni for me? She's still sleeping."

"Of course! What do you have in mind?"

"Another option. One we both might like." She continued down the hall. "Don't worry. I'll tell you all about it when I get back."

"Wait, Leann?"

"Yeah?" She paused at the door to her room.

"How will you get there? You don't have a car. And Michael's truck is gone. I have no idea where he went. He's acting strange."

Another thing she'd deal with today. But later.

"Um… I have no idea." There went her plan. Her spirits dropped to the floor.

"I'll drive you. Mom can keep an eye on Sunni."

"But it's Christmas Eve…"

"So? We have nothing going on until dinner tonight." She grinned. "Let me know when you're ready to leave."

"Give me ten minutes."

"You got it."

Leann hustled to her room. Michael was the real deal. She'd gotten so used to believing she couldn't trust men, she'd forgotten good ones were out there. And she'd been blessed to find one of the best. A future with Michael appealed to her more than anything. If he really was staying here, she'd do everything she could to stay here, too. She wanted a strong man by her side. A daddy for Sunni. A friend to share her ups and downs with.

She wanted a lasting love. And Michael was the only man for her.

Grabbing her phone, she texted Kelli.

First things first.

Get her job back.

Then claim her man.

* * *

Michael took long strides down the sidewalk outside the bakery. He held a box of doughnuts in one hand and a list in the other. He'd spent a restless night bogged down by confusion. After midnight, he'd finally prayed about his life. He'd thanked God for bringing him home for good. And he'd realized he'd needed six years to get over the betrayal of his brother and Kelli. Time had healed his broken parts.

He was finally free from the negative feelings that had kept him away from home in the past. He was ready to take a chance on love. With the right woman this time.

He was going to convince Leann to stay in Sunrise Bend. Once he did, he would spend as much time as necessary proving to her he was the guy she needed—one who would stick around for her and Sunni.

To do that, he needed to help her find a job.

He'd gotten up early, driven to town, grabbed a copy of the *Sunrise Sentinel* and asked every store open what jobs were available in town. The list in his hand held several options. He hoped Leann would consider staying.

Unlocking his truck, he stowed the doughnuts on the passenger seat. Glancing back through his rearview, he glimpsed Sunni's car seat. His throat grew tight. Towing her and Leann around had breathed new life into him. He loved the kid. And he loved her mama, too.

If Leann decided not to stay, he wasn't giving up on her. His relationship with his sister had thrived even though they'd lived far away from each other. He'd make a long-distance relationship work with Leann, too, if she'd let him.

She'd told him she liked him. Yesterday, he'd barely processed her words, but now that he'd had time to think about the way she'd looked at him and talked to him all week, he believed her. It filled him with hope.

He backed out of the parking spot and drove into the blinding sunlight on his way home. It was a beautiful Christmas Eve. It would be even better if his talk with Leann went well.

Lord, please grant me grace today. Let me get through to Leann. And no matter what, help me to trust Your plan for my life.

This Christmas was already shaping up to be the best one in years.

Chapter Thirteen

Michael burst into the kitchen with the box of doughnuts. His mom sipped coffee at the kitchen counter.

"Where have you been? You were out awfully early for Christmas Eve." She smiled at him. He set the box on the counter and kissed her cheek.

"Just out getting doughnuts." Frowning, he glanced around. "Where's Leann?"

What if she'd left? Packed her and Sunni's few belongings and left town? Wait, that didn't make sense. Her car was still in the shop.

"She and Hannah went out a little while ago. Sunni had breakfast then conked out on the couch while watching a cartoon. I think the ranch has worn that baby out."

Now that he had a plan to convince Leann to stay, he couldn't wait any longer to tell his mother about the ranch. "Hey, Ma, can I talk to you for a minute?"

"Uh-oh. I don't like your tone."

"You'll like this. I think you will, at least."

"Okay. What's up?"

"I have a little surprise for you."

"Ooh, I like surprises."

"I want to join Dad on the ranch. Dad and I discussed

it, and when he's ready to retire, I'll take it over for good. I'm moving back home."

Tears instantly formed in her eyes. "Oh, Michael, do you mean it? To think all three of my kids will be back here…" Choked up, she pressed her fist against her lips and shook her head, trying not to cry. Then she clasped her hands, raising her face to the ceiling. "Thank You, Jesus! You heard my prayers!"

One big teardrop slid down her cheek, then another, and she beamed, holding her arms wide open to him. He stepped into her embrace.

"God is so good, honey. I've been praying for an answer for the ranch's future and for your dad to not be so overworked, but never did I imagine God would send my own son as the answer to both prayers! This is cause to celebrate!" She looked around, grabbed another coffee mug and filled it to the brim. "Grab a doughnut, honey!"

Stunned, he suppressed a laugh.

"Cheers!" With her face flushed and eyes sparkling, she handed him the mug and clinked it with hers, then she took a huge bite of a chocolate-frosted doughnut.

"Myco? Where Mama?" Sunni toddled into the kitchen in kitty pajamas. She rubbed her eyes with one hand and held Bumbles with the other.

"Hey, cutie. Your mommy is with Hannah." He swung her up high in his arms. She giggled. "Want a doughnut?"

"Doughnut!"

"While you're settling down…" His mom grew serious and jerked her head toward Sunni. "You know I'm enjoying this little one and her mama."

"I'm working on that, too."

"Good." She winked. "Now, Miss Sunni, which doughnut would you like? The pink one with sprinkles or…"

At least one important conversation had gone well. Now

if he could get his pulse under control, maybe the next conversation would be a winner, too.

If Leann would just get here…

Leann wanted to pump both fists in the air and jump for joy, but she settled for getting into Hannah's car.

"Soo…?" Hannah shifted into Drive.

"We worked it out." After Hannah had dropped her off at Kelli's house, Leann had gotten to the heart of the matter. She'd asked Kelli if being a stay-at-home mom fulltime wasn't what she really wanted. And when Kelli hadn't answered, Leann had suggested easing into it on a parttime basis. Kelli's perfectly made up face had crumbled, and she'd admitted that Owen's colic had all but demolished her fantasy of being the perfect homemaker.

"Did she give you your job back?" Hannah headed back to the ranch.

"Not exactly, but we worked out an arrangement where we'll both be happy." Leann felt better than she had in a long time. Kelli still wanted to spend more time at home while limiting her hours at The Sassy Lasso. And Leann was relieved to work shorter hours for now.

"That's great, Leann! Does this mean you're staying?"

"Yes." She took in the open land and distant mountains. "I belong here."

"We're going to have so much fun. I'll help you move into your apartment." Hannah grinned.

"And I'll help you move into yours when you're ready."

"See? This is why I'm glad Michael found you. Mom and Dad act like I'm silly for wanting my own place."

"You're not silly, Hannah. You've grown up. It's okay. They'll get the memo eventually."

"I know, and I love them. They're so supportive. And wait until you experience Mom's Christmas food. Tonight's meal is just a warm-up for tomorrow, and trust me, you'll want your stretchy pants."

Leann laughed, but the closer they got to the ranch, the more her nerves began to spark and sizzle. One problem was solved, but the other one...

Would it be too much to expect it be resolved in a nice Christmas bow like her job had been?

Hannah pulled into the long driveway of the ranch. Leann clenched and unclenched her hands. Would Michael be there? Or would she have to wait even longer?

His truck came into view, and adrenaline raced through her veins.

He was here. And in a few minutes, she'd have to tell him what was on her heart.

Please, God, help me trust You. Help Michael listen to what I have to say.

As soon as Hannah parked, Michael came outside. Hannah waved to him, then frowned when she saw his serious expression.

"Uh, I'll leave you two alone." Hannah hurried inside.

"Michael—" Leann started to say, but as he strode toward her, she forgot her words.

He stopped a foot in front of her. "We have to talk."

"I know." She blinked, trying to gauge his mood. Was he mad at her? "I'm sorry for yesterday. I barely let you speak, and I made assumptions."

"You don't have to apologize." He stared at her intensely. "I'm not great at tough conversations."

Her heart sank a little lower. "I'm not, either, but sometimes they need to happen." *Fight for him, Leann!* She stood a little taller, lifted her chin. "Well, I hope this isn't a tough conversation. I hope it's easy."

"Oh, yeah?"

"Yeah, because I'm not leaving Sunrise Bend."

Michael looked stunned, and she wasn't sure if it was good or bad.

And it didn't matter, because in a split second, she was in his arms. As she looked up at him, she gasped. And she knew it was good.

Very good, indeed.

"You're staying?" His voice sounded like an old gravel road, and he didn't care. His arms wrapped around her waist, and her face was inches from his.

She nodded, those huge blue eyes twinkling, inviting.

"Good, because I spent the morning writing down every job opening in the area." He let go of her momentarily to fish for the list in his pocket. He handed it to her. She took it but didn't open it. "I want you to stay."

"You do?"

"Yep. I meant it yesterday. I'm not moving to Alaska. I'm ready to settle down, have a home. Have a family. And researching fish isn't going to get me there, Leann."

"What will you do?" Her words sounded breathless.

"Ranch. Right here. With my dad. I miss it. Miss him. Always loved working next to him."

"I'm so glad."

"Me, too. And that's not all. I…" He took a moment to get his composure. "There's no way to tell you this without you thinking I'm losing it, but I'm in love with you. I love you."

"You love me?" Her eyes grew watery. "From the minute I met you, you've been rescuing me. I never dreamed I'd find such a caring, strong man. And here you are. I thought for sure you were too good to be true."

"Me? Too good? Hardly." His chest was expanding to the point of bursting. "I thought I was pretty boring. I'm not exactly outgoing, and I get my thrills studying rivers and fish."

Her laugh tinkled through the air. "Well, I'm not a social butterfly. My life revolves around Sunni."

"And I love that about you." He pulled her closer to him.

"I love that you're so sweet with Sunni." She put her arms around his neck. "I don't know how, but I fell hard for you, and I can't let you go. I love you, too, Michael."

He couldn't believe she loved him! He got lost in her eyes. And he couldn't wait another minute. This woman was his. He lowered his mouth to hers, savoring her sweetness and the feel of her body curving against his. He could picture a lifetime of kisses right here on the family ranch.

She burrowed closer to him until he broke away from the kiss, still holding her tightly.

"I'm sorry about Kelli, you know. I didn't mean for you to think I was still in love with her. I wasn't. I'm not."

"I know. I hadn't realized how painful it must have been for you to have your brother swoop in and take her. Not to mention, she should have broken things off with you when she realized she was attracted to David. I don't blame you for avoiding them."

"You're right. I got over Kelli pretty quickly, but I couldn't get past David's betrayal. I was embarrassed. Angry. Bitter. That's why I avoided them. That's why it was awkward. But I think David and I are going to be okay now."

"You will be."

"You think so?" He wanted to kiss those lips again. So he did. And he quickly forgot where he was at—got lost in her soft embrace.

She placed her hands on his chest. "Oh! I didn't tell you. I talked to Kelli this morning. We worked it out." Her face beamed with joy.

"Worked what out?"

"I realized she had cold feet about giving up managing The Sassy Lasso and being a homemaker, and I think Owen's colic had a lot do with it. We discussed it and decided to co-manage the store."

He frowned. It sounded good, but was it the best option for Leann?

"Are you okay with it? Financially, I mean? There are other possibilities." He pointed to the list crumpled in her hand.

"Yeah, I am." Her big smile practically blinded him. "I'm glad I'll be able to spend more time with Sunni. I'm pretty frugal, so between my income and child support, I'll be okay."

He knew she'd be all right. He planned on putting a ring on her pretty left-hand finger as soon as possible. Snowflakes began to fall on them.

"Merry Christmas, Leann." He put his arm around her shoulder and turned her to the house. "I'm taking you back inside where it's warm."

"What will your mother think?"

"She'll think it's high time I settled down with a good woman."

She laughed again. "I never thought I'd say this, but I'm glad my car slid off the road into that sign."

"Welcome to Sunrise Bend, my love."

Epilogue

One year later...

Home sweet home. Michael let out a sigh of satisfaction as he took in the lodge's living room with the tall Christmas tree adorned with the glass fish ornaments Leann had bought him, then he smiled at the stuffed animals on the couch and wrapping-paper rolls propped in the corner.

"We're going to be late!" Leann hollered, trying to find Sunni's other black dress shoe. She lifted a shoe triumphantly. "Phew! Found it."

"We've got plenty of time." Michael put his arm around Leann's waist and tugged her to him. "Relax." He stole a kiss, and she smiled up at him.

"Being late might not be so bad." She cupped her hands around his face and kissed him back.

"Mommy! Daddy!" Sunni bounded downstairs from her bedroom and launched herself into Michael's arms.

"Whoa, there. You're not excited, are you?" He lifted her to sit on his hip.

"Let's go! I want to be Rachel's sheep." She wriggled to be set down, and he obliged. Then she allowed Leann to help her get her shoes on.

He and Leann had gotten married in June after a short engagement, and they'd moved into the newly remodeled lodge. It felt like home. Well, anywhere Leann and Sunni happened to be felt like home. Michael couldn't be happier.

"Give me one more minute." Leann shoved her arms into a coat and slung her purse over her shoulder. "Sunni, we need to zip you up."

The three-year-old was opening the door to the garage. Her coat dragged behind her. Michael shook his head, inwardly laughing. The kid got cuter every day. He loved her more than he thought humanly possible.

As they piled into his truck, he turned on a Christmas station.

"Just think," Leann said, "it was a year ago when you found us in the storm."

"I took one look at you, and my heart was toast."

She shot him a grin. "Mine, too. Have I told you I love you lately?"

"No," he teased, shooting her a sideways glance, as he headed to the main road.

"I guess it *has* been a few hours."

"Way too long."

"By the way, we have to help Hannah move into her new apartment next week."

"She's really moving out, huh?"

"Yep. She said as soon as she got hired full-time at the elementary school, she was getting her own place. And I told her not only would we help, we'd bring a few strong, single men."

"Why in the world would you tell her that?" He stiffened. "She doesn't need a bunch of guys in her apartment. She's fine on her own."

"Sure, she is." With a knowing smile, Leann patted his arm.

"Well, while you're off matchmaking, I'm going to help Dad check for pregnant cattle."

"You are not! You're going to help your sister."

"I guess you're right. Someone needs to be there to glare at any potential riffraff."

"On second thought, go help your dad check those cows."

He laughed.

They sat in easy silence for a few miles.

"It's funny, isn't it?" He glanced over at her. "Last year I had to be dragged to David's house after the children's nativity play, but this year, I can't wait to go."

"I know." She smiled. "I wanted it all last year—the house, the husband, the sense of belonging."

"And now?"

"I got it. All of it, and more. Because of you."

"You've got it all backward. You blessed me with all those things. I couldn't ask for more. You're the light of my life, Leann Carr."

"And you're the light of mine."

* * * * *

Don't miss Her Cowboy Till Christmas,
*the first book in Jill Kemerer's
brand-new miniseries,
Wyoming Sweethearts,
coming in December!*

Dear Reader,

Thank you for spending time in Sunrise Bend with me. I've always adored hero-to-the-rescue stories, probably because I've been in situations where I was alone and had no idea what to do. Who doesn't need a hero now and then? Leann found a man who valued her and Sunni, and what better way for her to meet Michael than in a snowstorm right before Christmas?

Although he didn't know it at first, Michael was ready to move past David's and Kelli's betrayal, and the Christmas season proved the ideal time for him to meet the woman of his dreams. He deserved someone who found him fascinating. I'm thrilled he got his happily-ever-after.

There have been many times in my life when I've felt misunderstood, boring or forgotten. I've grown so much closer to the Lord as a result. He understands me, doesn't think I'm boring and would never forget me. He feels the same about you. God loves us so much He sent His Son to save us. How blessed we are!

Have a very merry Christmas!

Jill Kemerer